THE EYE OF JADE

Diane Wei Liang was born in Beijing. She spent part of her childhood with her parents in a labour camp in a remote region of China. While attending Peking University in the 1980s, she took part in the Student Democracy Movement and was in Tiananmen Square. Diane has a PhD in Business Administration from Carnegie Mellon University and was a professor of management in the US and the UK for over ten years. She lives in London with her husband and their two children.

DIANE WEI LIANG

THE EYE OF JADE

A NOVEL

PICADOR

First published 2007 in Picador by Pan Macmillan Australia Pty Limited

First published in Great Britain 2007 by Picador

This edition first published 2008 by Picador
an imprint of Pan Macmillan Ltd
Pan Macmillan, 20 New Wharf Road, London N1 9RR
Basingstoke and Oxford
Associated companies throughout the world
www.panmacmillan.com

ISBN 978-0-330-45612-8

1 3 5 7 9 8 6 4 2

A CIP catalogue record for this book is available from
the British Library.

Printed and bound in Great Britain by
Mackays of Chatham plc, Chatham, Kent

For Andreas, Alexander, Elisabeth

and

for my mother, with love

1

In the corner of an office in an old-fashioned building in Beijing's Chongyang district the fan was humming loudly, like an elderly man angry at his own impotence. Mei and Mr Shao sat across a desk from each other. Both were perspiring heavily. Outside, the sun shone, baking the air into a solid block of heat.

Mr Shao wiped his forehead with a handkerchief. He had refused to remove his suit jacket. 'Money's not a problem.' He cleared his throat. 'But you must get onto it right away.'

'I'm working on other cases at the moment.'

'Do you want me to pay extra, is that it? You want a deposit? I can give you one thousand yuan right now.' Mr Shao reached for his wallet. 'They come up with the fakes faster than I can produce the real thing, and sell them at less than half my price. I've spent ten years building up my name, ten years of blood and sweat. But I don't want you talking to your old friends at the Ministry, you understand? I want no police in this.'

'You are not doing anything illegal, are you?' Mei wondered

why he was so keen to pay her a deposit. That was most unusual, especially for a businessman as shrewd as Mr Shao.

'Please, Miss Wang. What's legal and what's not these days? You know what people say: "the Party has strategies and the people have counter-strategies".'

Mr Shao stared at Mei with his thin eyes. 'Chinese medicine is like magic. Regulations are for products that don't work. Mine do. That's why people buy them.'

He gave a small laugh. It didn't ease the tension. Mei couldn't decide whether he was a clever businessman or a crook.

'I don't like the police – no offence, Miss Wang; I know you used to be one of them. When I started out, I sold herbs on the street. The police were always on my tail, confiscating my goods, taking me in to the station as if I was a criminal. Comrade Deng Xiaoping said *Ge Ti Hu* – that individual traders were contributors to building socialism. But did the police care for what he said? They're muddy eggs. Now things are better. I've done well and people look up to me. But if you ask me, the police haven't changed. When you need protection, they can't help you. I asked them to investigate the counterfeits. Do you know what they told me? They said they don't do that kind of work. But whenever there is a policy change, an inspection or a crackdown, you can bet they'd jump on me like a hungry dog.'

'Whether you like the police or not, we must play by the book,' Mei said, though her voice was less convincing than her words.

Private detectives were banned in China. Mei, like others in the business, had resorted to the counter-strategy of registering her agency as an information consultancy.

'Of course,' agreed Mr Shao. A smile as wide as the ocean filled his face.

*

After Mr Shao had left, Mei walked over to stand next to the fan. Slowly the faint breeze flowing through her silk shirt began to cool her.

The door opened. Mei's assistant, Gupin, looking like a cooked lobster, tumbled in. Without a word, he dashed over to his desk in the entrance hall and drained a glass jar of cold tea that had been there since morning. He slipped the army bag from his shoulder and dropped it on the floor.

'Was that Mr Shao, the King of Hair-Growth Serum, I saw leaving?' He looked up, catching his breath. He spoke with a faint but noticeable accent that gave him away as a country boy.

Mei nodded.

'Are you going to take his case?'

'I told him I would, but now I wonder. There is something odd about that man.'

'He wears a toupee.'

Gupin came over with a small packet wrapped in newspaper. 'I've collected five thousand yuan in cash from Mr Su.' He smiled. His face, still red from exertion, shone with pride.

Mei took the package and squeezed it gently. It felt firm. She made space for Gupin in front of the fan.

'Was he difficult?' she asked. Gupin was now standing next to her, his bare arm almost touching hers. She could smell his sweat.

'At first. But he can't scare me or distract me with his tricks. I've seen weasels like him before, and I've travelled many roads. People get worried when they see a migrant worker like me in that kind of place.' The word 'weasel' sounded especially nasty in Gupin's accent.

Mei smiled. At times like this, she couldn't help thinking how right she had been to hire him. And, oddly, she had her younger sister to thank.

When Mei had opened her agency, Lu, her younger sister, was critical of the idea. 'What do you know about business? Look at yourself – you don't socialise, you can't cope with politics, you have no *Guanxi* – none of the networks and contacts you need. How can you possibly succeed? Contrary to what you might think, my dear sister, running a business is tough. I know: I'm married to a successful businessman.'

Mei rolled her eyes. She was too tired to fight anymore. Since she had resigned from the Ministry for Public Security, everyone seemed to want to lecture her.

'Well, I suppose you are at the end of your ropes,' Lu sighed at last. 'If you can't hold on to your job at the Ministry, what else can you do? You might just as well work for yourself. But I can't watch you jump into a churning river without knowing how to swim. Let me find someone who can teach you the basics of business.'

The next day, Mr Hua had called to invite Mei to his office. There, she sat on a dark leather sofa and was served coffee by his pretty secretary while Mr Hua talked about *Guanxi*, about which procedures could be avoided and a few that couldn't, about creative organisation and accounting, and, most of all, about the importance of having sharp eyes and ears.

'You need to be sensitive to the change of wind and policy,' he said. 'Make sure you always watch out for people who might stab you from behind. And one word of advice –' Mei had quickly learned that 'one word of advice' was a favourite expression of Mr Hua – 'don't trust anyone who is not your friend. You want to succeed, then make sure you have a good *Guanxi* network, especially in high places.'

Mr Hua topped up his coffee for the fifth time. 'What about secretaries?' he asked Mei.

'What about them?'

'Have you thought about what kind of secretary you need?'

Mei told him that she had no plans to hire a secretary, not before she had any clients.

Mr Hua shook his head. 'You can hire someone for very little money. There are plenty of migrant workers from the provinces willing to work for almost nothing. The cost of having someone answer the phone or run errands is small, but the benefit is considerable. Your business won't look right without a secretary. If you don't look right, no one will come to you. Look around and tell me what you see.'

Mei looked around. The office was big and full of expensive-looking furniture. 'You've got a great place,' she said.

'Exactly. What I have here is what people call a "leather bag company". I invite foreign investors to become part of a joint venture. All foreign firms are required to have a Chinese partner, as you know. They come here to meet me, they see a grand set-up, the best address. But they don't realise that I have no factory or workforce of my own. They think I'm important, the real thing. I only go and find factories once I receive money from the foreign firm. If I can do one deal a year, I'm set. Two, I can take the rest of the year off.

'You see, making money is easy. The difficult part is getting people to pay up. That's why I like to do business with foreigners. It's much more difficult with the Chinese. One word of advice – when you hire someone, think about payment recovery and make sure your girl is tough enough to do the money chasing.'

Seeing the sense in what he was saying, Mei advertised for a secretary for her new business. Amongst all the applicants, Gupin was the only man. Mei had not considered hiring a man to be her secretary. But she decided to interview him.

Gupin had come from a farming village in Henan province and was working on Beijing's construction sites to get by.

'I finished top of the class at our county high school,' he told Mei in his Henan accent. 'But I had to go back to my village because that's where my official record was. I wanted to work in the county town, but my village head didn't agree. He said our village needed a "reading book man".'

It took Mei some time to get used to his accent and understand what he was saying.

'My ma wanted me to get married. But I didn't want to. I don't want to end up like my brother. Every day he gets up at dawn and works in the field all day. By the end of the year, he still can't afford to feed his wife and son. My da was like that too. He died long ago from TB. Everyone says there is gold in the big cities. So I thought I'd come to Beijing. Who knows what I can do here?'

Mei watched him. He was young, just turned twenty-one, with broad shoulders. Packs of muscle were visible under his shirt. When he smiled, he seemed bashful but honest.

Regretfully, she told him that he couldn't do the work she needed. He didn't know Beijing and his Henan accent would put people off.

'As soon as people hear your accent, they will assume many things about you and probably about this business too. Some people may even think that I'm running some sort of con. It's stupid, I know. That's how people are, though. The same would happen to me if I were to go to Shanghai. I'd probably be cheated by taxidrivers and given all the wrong directions.'

But Gupin was persistent. 'Give me a chance,' he begged her. 'I'm a quick learner and I work hard. I can learn about Beijing.

Give me three months and I promise I will know all the streets. I'll get rid of my accent too. I can, believe me.'

In the end, Mei decided to give him a chance. She remembered what Mr Hua had said and thought Gupin would make, if not a brilliant secretary, at least a more threatening debt collector than anyone else she had interviewed. He was also by far the cheapest.

'I'll give you a year,' she told him. 'You have no idea how big Beijing is.'

More than a year later, Gupin had proved to be everything he said he was: hardworking, smart and loyal. He had spent much of his spare time riding through the *hutongs* and streets of Beijing on his bicycle, and he now knew more about certain neighbourhoods than Mei did. He became another pair of ears and eyes for her.

'Well done,' Mei told Gupin. 'Mr Su is not the sort of man to part with money easily. Let's finish up.'

They packed up and checked all the locks on the door. It felt cooler in the dim corridor.

'I hope the weekend won't be as hot,' Gupin said as they walked out of the building. His military bag bounced over his shoulder. 'Are you doing anything special?'

'A picnic in the Old Summer Palace.'

'Going so far for a picnic?'

'It's my university class reunion.'

Outside, the sunshine was hazy and the air thick as syrup. The two of them said goodbye and parted, Gupin heading to a young aspen tree to which he had chained his Flying Pigeon bicycle and Mei to her two-door Mitsubishi, parked under an ancient oak tree.

2

That night, Mei was woken by a violent thunderstorm. The thin windows of her apartment rattled. Thunder cracked and roared, lightning flashed. The sound of rain flooded the space around her, calling to her mind lost thoughts and memories.

She thought about her old classmates, and who amongst them she might see the next day. She remembered Sparrow Li, the small gloomy boy who had played guitar. She thought of Guang, a foul-mouthed giant at six foot three. Big Sister Hui's round face came into her mind too. She remembered their cramped dorm room with its four bunk beds. She remembered the chestnut tree outside their window and the loudspeaker on one of its branches blasting out music at six-thirty every morning. She remembered how young they were.

Slowly the storm began to settle. The rain still poured, now monotonously. Mei tossed about in her bed. In her mind's eye, she saw the courtyard of a temple. It was getting dark and Guang was working a small petrol stove. It was the time her class had gone on a weekend trip to the West Mountains. It was before dawn and they trod carefully, using torches, along a path hanging over what they later saw in daylight to be a sheer drop of hundreds of metres. They held hands and followed each other's footsteps.

She was holding Yaping's hand. She could feel the warmth of his touch. Her thoughts drifted; in her dream she began to float. They reached the summit and the sun was shining. As they looked around them they saw nothing but endless mountains covered in red azaleas. Only now it wasn't Yaping's hand she was holding.

She was six years old. She was holding her father's hand.

They were walking down a long mountain trail, led by the guard of the labour camp. Behind them, tumbling like a lost leaf, lurched an old woman who had come to visit her son and who was now going home. She was to take Mei as far as Qunming, the capital of Yunnan. There Mei would be met by an acquaintance of her mother's who was going to Beijing by train.

Over his shoulder, Mei's father carried a grey bundle containing Mei's possessions – her clothes, two labour camp standard-issue hand towels, a toothbrush, an aluminium mug, and small toys made from wire, cardboard and toothpaste caps. There was also a notebook her father had made from yellowed paper he had found. Inside, he had written Tang poems from memory. Mei had carefully pressed the leaves she had collected between the pages.

They chatted, as fathers and daughters do, about the time they had spent together and the time they would share again. Mei ran her fingers through the azaleas they passed, making the red flowers dance happily like butterflies.

At midday, they reached the dirt road at the bottom of the mountain. By the side of a cliff, a cold waterfall jetted into a small pool and then through a half-buried concrete pipe down to the river below. They waited by the waterfall. Birds sang from beyond the trees. Along the cliffs ablaze with the bright colours of the south, the road stretched in front of them.

How long does the road go on? Mei wondered. How far do the trees, the giant mountains and the river go on?

Time ticked away unhurriedly. An old bus appeared in the distance. They watched it draw closer and closer until finally it halted noisily in front of them.

Mei's father handed the bundle to the bus driver, who put it on top of the bus with other luggage.

The old woman, whom Mei was told to call Old Mama, held her hand.

'Don't worry, Comrade Wang. Little Mei will be fine with me.' Old Mama started to board the bus.

But Mei's father did not let her go. 'Tell your mother and sister that I miss them. Tell them I will be back soon.'

'Bus is going!' shouted the driver, climbing into his cab.

Old Mama hurriedly pulled Mei on board.

'Be a good girl, Mei,' cried her father. 'Listen to Old Mama. I'll see you in Beijing! I promise.'

The bus started to cough and shake. Mei ran to the muddy back window and knelt on the wooden seat. She feverishly waved her tiny arms.

'Goodbye,' she screamed, smiling wide as if the sun were inside her and would always shine. 'See you in Beijing, Baba!'

The road began to pull her father and his guard away, first slowly as he waved, and then faster. Finally they shrank into two lost figures. The green cliffs leaned over as if about to crush them. Then the bus turned the corner. They were gone.

Mei woke up. Blinding sunlight had stormed in to the little apartment she rented by the busy ring-road. She had never seen her father again after they said goodbye on that dirt road twenty-three years ago.

Mei turned her head to look at the black alarm clock ticking on her nightstand. It was late. But she couldn't get up. She felt that she had been drained of her will. Next to the clock was a small black-and-white portrait of her father. The photo had faded over the years. After Baba died, Mama had thrown away all his things – his manuscripts, his photos and his books. This portrait was all Mei was able to save. She had carried it with her, hidden inside a copy of *Jane Eyre*, to boarding school and university. She didn't show anyone the photo, nor did she talk about her father. It was her secret, her pain and her love.

Mei saw her father smiling at her from inside the picture frame. She heard her heart beating an echoless beat. She thought about the happiness that could have been.

The thunderstorm had brought fresh air and a comfortable temperature to the shoppers packing the pavement along College Road. Clothing stores, hair salons and supermarkets enticed passers-by with new styles and discounts. Fruit and vegetable vendors, their goods piled high on flatbed carts, shouted out prices. A peasant woman in wide-legged trousers waved a straw fan over a heap of watermelons. The flies had returned too.

Stopped by the traffic light at Three Village Junction, Mei tapped her fingers on the steering wheel. She couldn't afford to stop; she was terribly late. She had spent too much time washing, drying and styling her long straight hair. She had put on make-up and then taken it off again.

Why did she even care? She shook her head. She never had when she was at university. Then, she was an outsider who never wanted to be in. What had changed?

At the end of College Road, Mei turned north along the high walls of Qinghua University. The traffic had thinned. Cyclists rode at a leisurely pace in the shade of the aspen trees. Mei passed a group of students on their bicycles. It looked like they were going to the West Mountains for the weekend.

She remembered travelling on this very road as a student herself. Peking University, her alma mater, and Qinghua University were sister universities, so by tradition Mei's class was linked with a friendship class consisting of forty-five electrical engineers from Qinghua University. The engineers, mostly men, enthusiastically organised friendship disco parties; there were a lot of girls in Mei's class. She remembered sitting on the back of Yaping's bicycle, her long hair flying in the wind. There was warmth in the air on those nights, and the stars flickered like eyes. Street lamps glowed softly through the jasmine-scented breeze. The night was pure and crickets sang under the pagoda by Weiming Lake.

Over the years, Big Sister Hui had brought her news of Yaping: he got married; he finished his MBA; he started working; he bought a house.

From time to time, she still thought about him, tried to imagine him dressed in a business suit, riding the 'L' train. She wondered whether he still wore the same pair of black-rimmed glasses. Sometimes she remembered his intelligent eyes and shy smile. When she hated him, she imagined him old, no longer slender or gentle. But most of the time, she couldn't picture him at all. The names didn't mean anything to her: Chicago, Evanston, North Shore. She had no image of them, nor could she picture Yaping's wife or their life together. She turned onto Qinghua West Road and caught sight of the Old Summer Palace.

Since their graduation, Big Sister Hui had organised yearly

reunions. Big Sister Hui had stayed in the department, first as a graduate student and then as a lecturer. At first Mei didn't go to the reunions because she didn't want to talk about Yaping or their break-up. Then she was too busy. After her boss was promoted, Mei, as his personal assistant, moved into the favoured circle. She was allocated a one-bedroom apartment and high-profile responsibilities. She became desirable in the eyes of matchmakers. They introduced her to sons of high-ranking officials and rising stars of the diplomatic services. She went with them to restaurants, concerts, movie premieres and state banquets. She sat with their parents in airy apartments overlooking Renaissance Boulevard. She spent her spare time getting to know them so they could get to know her.

But everything had changed when she resigned from the Ministry. People with whom she had worked for years and thought of as friends shunned her.

Maybe this was why she cared so much about today, thought Mei, about how she looked and what her classmates might think of her. These people were her old friends. Though she had never seemed to need them before, she needed them now.

3

Big Sister Hui was waiting for her at the main entrance of the Old Summer Palace.

'I can't believe it! You, the person who has the luxury of a car, are late. We've been waiting for forty minutes. Ding had to take Little Po inside so that she could have a run around. A four-year-old kid is like a dog. If she doesn't get her run in the park, she bites.'

Big Sister Hui had lost weight, showing curves that Mei had not known she possessed. She was clearly pleased with her new shape and had wrapped it in a tight-fitting dress of rainbow colours.

'I'm sorry,' Mei apologised. 'I overslept.'

'It's the undisciplined life of a singleton. You ought to get married. It would do you good.'

Big Sister Hui took Mei's arm and they walked into the park like old girlfriends, hand in hand. A light breeze skipped across the long grass in the dried-up lake. Somewhere in the woods broken columns stood, half-hidden. Further on, piles of fallen stones were scattered by the winding paths. Before it was burned down by British and French troops during the Second Opium War two hundred years ago, scholars had likened the Old Summer Palace to Versailles. Mei had seen pictures of Versailles in books, yet standing amongst the ruins she could never imagine the palace's former splendour.

'So, how is life, princess?' Big Sister Hui was jolly as usual.

'Why do you always call me "princess"?'

'Well, if you had married any of your princes of revolution while you were at the Ministry . . .'

'Not that again.'

'Okay, okay.' Big Sister Hui put up her hands in surrender. 'Tell me about your work.'

'Work is going well. So many people come to see me for this and that. I think there are two things that people have too much of these days: money and affairs.'

'I'm not surprised. Rich people are everywhere. Just look at the traffic. Motorbikes were the big deal when we were in university. Remember Lan? She had a boyfriend who had a motorbike and we all thought he was a criminal.'

They both laughed.

'I'm glad things are finally going well for you,' Big Sister Hui said. 'What a terrible ordeal you had to go through at the Ministry. You didn't deserve that.'

Mei nodded and tried to smile.

The road forked out. They left the path and went up a small hill. Climbing soon made them hot. 'What a heat! It's only spring. The old sky is certainly messed up this year,' Big Sister Hui panted. Mei felt the dry grass being crushed beneath her feet. When they reached the top of the slope, they looked down on a meadow in the valley. A group of people was assembled there, sitting on plastic sheets.

'This is where we came to celebrate our graduation,' said Big Sister Hui, basking in the sunshine. 'Do you remember?'

A large shell-shaped stone that had once belonged to an ancient, ornate fountain stood in the middle of the meadow. Its white marble gleamed.

'Of course,' said Mei softly.

Suddenly the memory of that day was with her again. They were sitting around the remains of a picnic, smoking cigarettes and singing. Sparrow Li played guitar. Yaping read one of his poems . . .

'Hey!' someone shouted from the party, dragging her mind back to the present.

'It's Fat Boy.' Big Sister Hui waved and they started down the hill.

Sparrow Li was sitting on the plastic sheet, smoking, drinking beer out of a can and playing guitar. He looked even smaller and thinner than Mei remembered. His face, which had never looked young, now clearly showed age.

'You are late.'

'It's not my fault. It's the princess here.' Big Sister Hui flung her round body onto the sheet and pointed a finger at Mei.

'Big Sister Hui!' protested Mei.

Fat Boy said hello to the newcomers and offered them drinks. Mei took a bottle of water.

'How are you, Li?' She sat down next to Sparrow Li, causing him to blush.

Everyone knew that Sparrow Li had always been in love with Mei.

'I'm going to Shenzhen. I've had enough of Beijing and Xinhua News Agency,' Sparrow Li declared.

'What?' Fat Boy shouted. 'You didn't tell me! You are giving up the steel bowl for a private local newspaper? Are you out of your mind?'

'What's so great about Xinhua News Agency? We have no housing and the pay is lousy. When we graduated, it was all about getting a job with the big ministries. Now it's about money. If you are rich, you are somebody. I'm going to be the chief editor and make a lot of money.'

'Don't be naïve.' Big Sister Hui popped open a can of Qing Tao Beer. 'What's money compared to power? Mei had a beautiful one-bedroom apartment when she worked for the Ministry for Public Security. She travelled in official cars and dined in the best restaurants. She wasn't rich but didn't she live a good life! Look at your chief. He doesn't need to be rich. He gets everything he needs and more from his job.'

'Well, I'm never going to be the chief of Xinhua News Agency. It takes a special kind to climb the power pole. It's not me. I am going to be rich. I'll have my own car and my own apartment.'

'I don't need a car. But I would like to have a roof over my head.' Fat Boy sighed. '*Beijing Daily* is much worse than Xinhua News Agency. It doesn't even give me a dorm room. I'm thirty years old and still living with my parents. So I told the matchmakers that I'm only interested in girls whose work units have housing.'

'In Special Economic Zones like Shenzhen, people like us will be able to afford our own apartments.' Sparrow Li puffed on his cigarette.

'What about your Beijing residence?' Mei asked Li. 'You'll lose it if you leave. Don't you ever want to come back?'

Mei felt sad. Sparrow Li was always the hopeless, suffering romantic. He did things out of passion, sometimes without due consideration. Because of it, he never fitted in with the pragmatic Chinese way of life. In some ways, Mei felt a close connection to him. They were both outsiders, albeit different types. Sparrow Li longed for approval and acceptance by others. Mei, on the other hand, thought that no one understood her, and so didn't care about what they thought of her.

'Who doesn't want to come back?' a thick voice roared from behind them.

Everyone turned around and saw Guang's six-foot-three frame and black-smudged face towering over them. He had been working on the little petrol stove on the other side of the stone shell.

'It's Sparrow Li. He is going to Shenzhen,' said Fat Boy, shaking his head.

'Good for him,' said Guang, sitting down. He fanned Sparrow Li's cigarette smoke back into his face. 'You'll finally be with people your own size.' He laughed at his own joke.

Although Sparrow Li came from the land of giants – the northern province of Dongbei – he was the smallest in their class.

Big Sister Hui smacked Guang's back. 'Don't be an ass.'

The blow produced no effect. Guang laughed again. 'But don't think about running over to Hong Kong. Hong Kong is coming back to the motherland in a few months, so we'd catch you.'

Guang's wife produced a can of beer. He opened it, took a sip and spat. 'You didn't chill it like I told you!'

'It was chilled when I bought it,' his little wife answered. She spoke in a slight voice, avoiding his eyes.

'Get me a bottle of water!' he shouted at her.

At last, Big Sister Hui's husband, Ding, came with Little Po and the food bags. They had to navigate the hill slowly with the laden bicycle. Guang's wife cheered up and went to unload the food to make lunch. Ding chatted with her by the stove. Little Po wanted to play with her mama, so Big Sister Hui took her to find flowers in the grass.

The rest of them spread out plates, bowls, chopsticks, cold cuts, steamed buns and cooked rice. When Guang went to find his cigarettes, Mei followed him.

At the time of their graduation eight years ago, the Building Hainan Project was just taking off. The government's plan was to build the nation's biggest free economic zone on the island of Hainan, with five-star hotels, international resorts and modern industries. Guang, being an enthusiastic Party member, answered the first call and went to Hainan straight after graduation. The experience had made him bitter.

'Guang, why do you treat your wife like that?'

Guang lit a cigarette and puffed. 'Ah, I shouldn't have married her.' He leaned against a young aspen tree. 'I was wasting my life in Hainan. We met and I thought at least if I got married I'd have achieved one thing. I can understand what Sparrow Li is doing. I've done that, I've chased money. For heaven's sake, I spent six years in Hainan. Get rich? Bull! No one got rich except the damn officials. There was so much corruption that millions of yuan just disappeared. If you were a little guy like me, what did you get? Six years of your life gone and a wife you can't stand.'

'That's not your fault. The whole Hainan project was corrupt.'

'That's no consolation to me, is it?'

Mei shook her head. 'No. But is battering your wife any consolation?'

'Oh, bull.' Guang threw his cigarette down. 'Why can't you be kind for once? Give me a little sympathy.' He ground out the cigarette with his foot and strode off.

When lunch and beer were ready on the picnic sheet, they all gathered around and ate to their hearts' content.

The sun had risen high in the sky. The day was becoming hotter.

The old classmates swapped news about life and work. Under the watchful eye of Big Sister Hui, everyone avoided the topic of Mei's departure from the Ministry for Public Security. Mei smiled at her friend and thanked her with her eyes.

'Lan will be coming later,' Big Sister Hui informed them.

'Is she the rich mistress?' Guang's little wife asked.

Guang ignored her.

'I ran into her once at the Lufthansa Centre. She had loads of shopping bags and her chauffeur was carrying them for her.'

'I've met her man,' nodded Big Sister Hui. 'He's special, someone who is going to do very well one day, maybe like Mei's brother-in-law. He bought an apartment for Lan and another one for her parents. Her parents have moved to Beijing now.'

'See, this is what I mean,' exclaimed Sparrow Li. 'You don't need a job with a Beijing residence if you have money. You can buy your own apartment and pay for your own health care.'

'But is he going to marry her?'

'Oh, Mei,' laughed Big Sister Hui. 'He already has a wife and daughter.'

'Is she pretty? Lan, I mean. She must be,' said the little wife.

'Not as pretty as Mei,' said Fat Boy.

'Then how did she get so lucky?' shrieked the little wife.

'Good question,' they all murmured.

'For goodness sake, stop envying her. Is there no one here who thinks this is wrong?' Mei cried.

'I don't see anything wrong.' Guang sat up. 'She is well educated, intelligent and good for his business. He obviously appreciates her. The wife benefits too. The more successful her husband gets, the better off she is. If it doesn't work out, Lan gets to keep her apartments and money. It's a good arrangement, if you ask me.'

From beyond the woods, a breeze had picked up the sweet scent of pine oil and spring leaves. Fat Boy lay down on his back and traced the travelling clouds. Sparrow Li played Spanish love songs on his guitar.

Mei thought again about the time of their graduation, when they had come to this meadow. They were young and pure, their hearts filled with ideals. They had dreams and were ready for the world. They sang the first Chinese rock-n-roll hit, Cujian's 'I Have Nothing'.

She truly had nothing back then, not a car or a business or an apartment to herself. But she was happy. She was in love.

4

Driving home from the reunion, Mei could not get Yaping out of her mind. Having seen their old friends after so long seemed to have made his absence, which she thought she had buried, sharp again.

Mei had noticed Yaping on the first day of university. He was a surprisingly tall boy from the south, with sensitive eyes, a shy smile and soft hair that fell over his forehead. It did not take long for everyone to see that Yaping was the most talented in their class.

Mei and Yaping started going out in their third year. They discussed literature by Weiming Lake. They took trips to the West Mountains to visit temples and shrines. They went shopping to Wangfujing and Xidan, to browse through books and eat traditional Beijing specialities. They watched movies in the university hall, the best place in Beijing to see both imported and avant-garde Chinese films. Together they saw *Love Story* and *Roman Holiday*, the only two films from non-communist countries. After *Red Sorghum* won the Golden Bear at Berlin, director Zhang Yimou took his film to Peking University. Following the showing, the director and his leading actress came on stage. Mei still remembered how beautiful Gong Li looked and how everyone cheered.

But Mei's mother, Ling Bai, did not approve of Yaping. She thought him good-looking – 'in a soft southern river-town boy way' – and very bright, but he came from the provinces, which meant he would most likely have to go back there after graduation. Ling Bai would never have allowed Mei to move out of Beijing.

Ling Bai was a painter who worked in the art department of a propaganda magazine called *Women's Life*. She was an ordinary employee who had gained seniority in her old age, if not authority. Although Ling Bai had little ambition for herself, she expected her daughters to succeed. She might have been able to overlook Yaping's residency problem, for with luck and talent he might be allocated a job in Beijing. But he could not change his upbringing. His parents were merely schoolteachers. Yaping was not someone who could give Mei prospects and protection.

'One cannot live long on a diet of poetry,' Mama told Mei.

But Mei went on seeing Yaping anyway. They were in love.

In their last year at university, Yaping won a scholarship from the University of Chicago. After they graduated, he went to America. At first, his letters were long and enthusiastic. Then they became shorter, more infrequent. A year later, after not having written for a long time, Yaping wrote to tell Mei that he had fallen in love with someone else.

'I told you so,' said Mama. She was sitting in a folding chair on the balcony of her apartment with a cup of green tea. 'Now you see that I was right to be against it, don't you? I only wish you had listened to me. You are like your ba, too romantic.'

It was typical of Mama, thought Mei, clenching the steering

wheel. Mama was good at making her feel that she could do nothing right.

Before the Cultural Revolution ended and Mama was given the job at the magazine, they moved around a lot, following her temporary jobs and temporary housing. Mama became more fragile each time they moved. Mei and her sister learned not to do things that disturbed her. These might include noise, silence, things not in their proper place, dirt and bad news. But no matter how careful they were, Mama still cried.

It seemed to Mei that only her sister could make their mother smile. Lu was three years younger and extremely beautiful from an early age. She was sweet, charming and talented. Lu's teachers had only the best things to say about her. She was always praised as special, intelligent and kind. Mama loved her so much that Mei thought that she had no more love left for her elder daughter.

So it was a relief for everyone when Mei went to boarding school, though even there she stood out as not fitting in. This became clear to Mei when Ling Bai was summoned to the school to see Mei's class mother. Mei sat outside Mrs Tang's office, bored because Mama had been inside for a long time. What could they be talking about?

She tiptoed to the door and put her ear to the keyhole. She heard the voice of Mrs Tang. 'Mei is a good student. But it is unhealthy for a girl of her age to be alone all the time.'

'I am afraid she's got her father's temperament,' said Mama. 'He was a solitary person, the type who lived his life through literature, ideals and principles. He was a brilliant writer. But he didn't understand how the world worked. Eventually, his personality destroyed him. Whenever I see Mei, I see her father.

They have the same eyes. She's even got his expressions. I am scared. I try to help her, but she won't change. My other daughter, Lu, is not like this. She's good with people and understands everything automatically. I don't know why Mei is so different. Not because of anything I did, I hope. I love them both and treat them the same. Yet Mei has turned out just like her father – always looking down on others, always judging. It is as if no one is good enough. No one is up to her standards.'

'Perhaps you could take her to see a herbalist,' suggested Mrs Tang. 'They know how to soothe the temperament.'

'If only they could,' said Mama.

When Mei heard her mother coming towards the door, she ran back to her seat.

The herbs and the reading of *Qi* did not help. Mei continued to live in a world of her own, surrounded by her books and her thoughts. She read everything she could find. She wanted to be a writer like her father.

'Absolutely not.' Her mother put her foot down. 'How can you even think of being a writer? Writing is the most dangerous profession in China. Whenever there is a political movement, writers are always the first to go to jail.'

But Mama couldn't stop Mei; nor could she convince her that pragmatism was better than principles.

They had been in her mother's living room when Mei told Ling Bai that she had resigned from the Ministry for Public Security.

Mei had shrugged her shoulders, trying to look light-hearted. 'I will be fine. There are plenty of private companies out there. I will have no trouble finding a job. I can make more money.'

'But you won't have the same kind of future. Don't you know that power is all that matters? When you got that job at the

Ministry, I was so happy and relieved, to tell the truth. You know how I felt about your determination to be a writer or a journalist. I was glad that you didn't have to be either. I thought finally you were safe and I could stop worrying about you. But once again you prove me wrong.'

Mama paced in front of Mei. 'There must be something in you that is self-destructive. All those perfectly fine young men you were introduced to, not a single one worked out. Why?' She stopped moving and stared at her daughter. 'What happened to all the things I told you about? *Guanxi* networks? Compromise? Has it all gone in one ear and out the other?'

Mei bit her lips until they hurt.

'You could really learn from Lu,' said Mama.

Mei couldn't stay quiet. 'I'm not like Lu. You must know that by now. Frankly, I don't want to be like her. I don't want to be anybody's pretty pillow.'

'That's a horrible thing to say about your sister.'

'How much do you think she loved those boyfriends of hers? How much do you think she loves Lining? She loves his money.'

'You're jealous because she's happy.'

'She's happy because she lives for the moment and loves only herself.'

'That's not fair. No one asked you to carry a burden. I sacrificed my life so that you could have it easy – good school, nothing to worry about. But you choose to make life hard for yourself. All your principles and morals, what good are they if they can't make you happy?'

Mei tried to find a retort but the words stuck in her throat like fishbones. She got up from the sofa and walked to the window. Below, someone was coming out from the bicycle parking hut. Mei watched him get on his bike and ride away. She watched the empty afternoon. She saw the same story repeating itself – the odd child, the disobedient daughter, the failure.

'You are just like your father. You must act big. You set yourself up on a pedestal. You don't care about who you hurt.'

'If anyone, I hurt only myself.'

'You hurt me, your mother. I'm worried about you.'

A violent urge stirred inside Mei like never before. She turned around. All the anger and betrayal she had felt exploded. 'Then I ask you to stop worrying about me. I can take care of myself. I learned to do that when I was five, thanks to you. Have you any idea what it was like for me to see my father being beaten up and humiliated every day? If you really worried about me, you wouldn't have left me in the labour camp. You wouldn't have left Baba there to die.'

'How dare you? You – you ungrateful little beast! You have no right to judge me.' Mama began to shake, her voice cracking with suppressed tears. 'What do you know about love? All you do is read books. You think life is like a novel. No, reality is much darker than that. I didn't abandon you or your ba. If I could have taken you out, I would have. But I could only take one child with me and your sister was just two years old and very sick . . .'

Tears rolled down her cheeks.

'I got you out eventually, didn't I? You don't know how difficult it was. But you've never appreciated it. I gave up so much for you and Lu. All I want is for you to be happy. But look at what you've done.'

What indeed? Mei asked herself, turning off College Road. Was her mother right about her? Was she really the assassin of her own happiness? But no – as difficult as it had been to leave the Ministry, she couldn't have stayed. There can be no place for lies in true happiness, she asserted. As she turned onto the ring-road and saw, in the distance, the Gate of Moral Victory, she decided that she had done nothing wrong and that she would waste no more of the weekend brooding about the past.

5

Two weeks later, the heatwave was gone. Cold wind blew again from the north. The residents were warned of another yellow sandstorm.

Mei was in her office writing up the notes on the Mr Shao case. She was happy. As she put down the last word, she reflected warmly on the interest and variety her work brought.

The telephone rang in the entrance hall. A few minutes later, Gupin stuck his head through the small opening of the door. 'A Mr Chen Jitian just called. He'd like to come and see you tomorrow. He says he is a friend of your family.'

'Yes, he is.' Mei's eyes lit up.

'I've made the appointment. He will be here in the morning.'

'Very good.'

Mei leaned back in her chair and thought for a moment. She smiled. She was delighted to hear from Uncle Chen, though at the same time wondered why he wanted to see her. She looked out of the window. The sky was dark. The wind lashed at bare tree branches. She thought of the last time she'd seen

Uncle Chen, one and a half years ago, on a beautiful autumn day.

It is said that a daughter grows up and changes eighteen times, and the more she changes, the more beautiful she becomes. This was certainly true of Lu. By the time she met Lining when she was twenty-five, she had turned out to be, in the words of her future husband, possibly the most beautiful woman in Beijing. Yet her beauty was only part of her story; she was smart, too. She had studied psychology at university and was considered to be one of the best students in her class.

After graduation, Lu was assigned to work in Beijing Mental Hospital. She hated that job. After a year, she left the hospital, first to teach at the university she had so recently graduated from, and then to join the Ministry of Propaganda.

Her swift moves from one job to another were nothing short of miraculous, given that changes like this had to be approved by the central government as special cases. But Lu was the kind of special person on whom good fortune always seemed to be bestowed.

Her job at the Ministry of Propaganda landed her in the media. Soon she became a guest psychologist for Beijing TV. It was in one of Beijing TV's studios that Lu met Lining, an industrialist, who was appearing on the same program.

Three weeks before her wedding, Lu took Mei and her mother to Dim Sum at the famous Grand Three Element Restaurant.

It was a Tuesday morning. The restaurant was nearly empty. Aside from the Wang family, there were only two other customers: a Cantonese-speaking couple who were probably guests of the nearby Shangri-La Hotel. Streams of waitresses – dressed in traditional embroidered figure-hugging *Qi Pao* dresses with high mandarin collars and side-slits – did the rounds with food trolleys.

Over tiny steamers of curried snails, red oil beef tripe and prawn dumplings, the Wang women discussed the seating arrangements for the honoured guests at Lu's wedding.

'I want people to remember my wedding for years to come,' Lu announced. 'I want them to talk about it as one of the classiest events. I'm not going to copy the Deputy Mayor's daughter. Do you know that her father shut down the entire route to her wedding so that she could have a hundred-car parade? And then she had five thousand guests at her reception.

'My wedding will be different. I have limited the guest list to four hundred people, so it will be the most exclusive wedding of the year. Only the powerful, famous and wealthy have been invited.'

'That's as it should be,' Mama endorsed.

Another trolley arrived. Mama picked her favourite salted fish and peanut porridge. Mei chose a steamer of Dragon Buns.

'How is your new apartment?' Mei asked her sister.

Lining had bought a penthouse apartment near the Embassy District. It was being renovated by the best construction company in Beijing, according to Lu.

'It will be ready when we get back from our honeymoon. Did I tell you that they're doing it for free?'

You did, thought Mei.

'The chairman said that it's going to be his wedding present to us – isn't that sweet?' Lu smiled. 'Lining has so many friends and they all adore him and want to help.

'When we go to Europe, Lining said to me that I must go to all the shops. He knows that I love beautiful things. But a shopping honeymoon, how dreadful. "No," I told him, "I want to see the sights and go to museums." I can't wait to see the Eiffel Tower, Big Ben and the Colosseum.

'Besides, I told Lining that I can't shop even if I want to. We're already running out of space as it is: so many wedding gifts – Chinese antiques, modern Italian furniture, German appliances. Where will I put the new things? The sad truth is, some of the stuff that we have been given is really not to my taste. Don't get me wrong, they are perfectly wonderful, absolutely top of the line. But often I would have preferred a different colour or style.'

Lu spoke of her new life, waving her hands in excitement. Her fingers – slender, perfectly manicured – expressed her sensuality, as well as seeming to evoke the memory of a first kiss, or the aura of a girl becoming a woman.

She was wearing a long white dress. Just below the line of her breast, yards of chiffon were gathered and tied together with velvet ribbons. When she moved, these secret folds drew apart to reveal faint contours, a veiled suppleness that had been hidden before.

A food trolley once again lined up beside their table. Lu, teeth white and complexion radiant, leaned over to check the selections.

'Chicken feet,' she ordered.

The waitress removed the lid and placed the steamer on their table. She drew a stroke on the order slip and left.

'Oh, Mama, I almost forgot. Yesterday, Lining gave me another present.'

'What is it?' Mei saw Mama's face light up.

Lu tilted her head to the side, biting her lips. Then she swung back up, eyes shining like stars, and said, 'An imported Mercedes-Benz.'

'Bravo!' Ling Bai clapped her hands together in a praying

gesture. Her smile was as broad as that of her favourite daughter's.

'Isn't he wonderful, Mama?'

'It's obvious that he loves you very much,' said Ling Bai, patting Lu's hand.

'But what about your Mitsubishi?' Mei asked, spitting out a tiny bone from the chicken feet.

Lu had a small red two-door car that had been given to her by a previous boyfriend.

'I don't know. I haven't thought about it.' Lu stopped shifting her chopsticks.

Ling Bai frowned at her older daughter, who was, as usual, pouring cold water on a hot plate.

'Do you want it? I will give it to you,' Lu suddenly said cheerfully.

After hearing her own words, she felt pleased and quickly carried on with the idea. 'Yes, you take it and do something with your life. Maybe you can . . .' She raised her eyes to the ceiling in thought. 'Maybe you can drive around Beijing solving crime.'

She laughed.

Lu was only joking, but her words were more accurate than she realised. For some time now, Mei had been considering setting up her own business, a detective agency. The idea had come to her while she looked for work in the private industry. She had seen the freedom and prosperity entrepreneurship could bring.

A detective service was a natural choice for her. She had worked for years in the Ministry for Public Security – the police headquarters – in the thick of criminal investigations. And she had always loved Sherlock Holmes books. As a child, she had even fantasised about being a detective like Holmes.

Having her own detective agency would give her the independence she had always longed for. It would also give her the chance to show those people who shunned her that she could be successful. The more she thought about it, the more she was convinced that she could make money with her agency. People were getting rich. They owned properties, money, business and cars. With new freedom and opportunities came new crimes. There would be much that she could do.

6

Lu had considered holding her wedding ceremony on the eighth of August, a double lucky date because the number eight, *Ba*, rhymed with 'getting rich', *Fa*. But Lu hated the heat, which could be wicked in August. So she checked with a Feng Shui master who confirmed that the eighth of August of the Lunar Year was in fact luckier. For 1995, the eighth of August of the Chinese calendar fell in September.

The arrangements had been planned over several months, with many changes made along the way. At first Mei was going to be the head bridesmaid, and then she wasn't. Mei understood; of course she was Lu's sister, but the wedding was going to be a big event, with cameras and TV crews. Wei Wei, the movie star, would be more *Pai Chang*. She would bring more glory on the big day.

Two days before the wedding, Lu called.

'Sorry that I am doing this on the phone. There is still so much to do and on top of that, a crisis – the chef of the restaurant has left for the new Beyond Ocean. I went over there today and told

Mr Zhang that he'd better have his old chef cooking for my guests on Saturday. You know the kind of people who are coming to the wedding. I can't have some unknown chef. "It just won't cut it," I said to Mr Zhang. This is the trouble with restaurants in Beijing these days: something new is opening up every month. You can't catch up fast enough with the next hip thing.'

Mei said nothing. She did not know much about restaurants now that she no longer worked for the Ministry.

'I've been thinking and also talking to Mama about this. You know that I'm sorry for what happened to you at the Ministry, whatever the truth might be.'

'What do you mean, whatever the truth? There is only one truth; I am the one telling the truth.' Mei heard her own voice rise.

'This isn't coming out right. No, both Mama and I are absolutely on your side! Of course we believe you. All I am saying is that other people may not see it the way we do. You can't convince them either. Anyway, we thought perhaps you'd rather not want the attention of being a bridesmaid. People may talk and speculate as to why you left the Ministry. You don't want that.'

'You are inviting my old boss, aren't you?'

'My dear sister, if it were up to me, I'd cut his filthy pigtail off for you. But I can't withdraw the invitation. I am sure you understand; he is not someone you want to make an enemy of.'

'This doesn't exactly sound like you're on my side,' retorted Mei. 'How long have you and Mama being planning this? Ever since I left the Ministry?'

'I am sorry, Mei. We would hate to see you get hurt, that's why we think it would be better if you keep a low profile on Saturday. Lower your head just once, please – for me, for your little sister's wedding day.' Lu's voice sounded as if it had been dipped in honey. 'You know that there is little I can do, don't you? I can't even put your ex-boss upstairs. I would have liked to, believe me.'

Mei felt like crying.

'Mei, don't forget there are still others that you hate, like Mrs Yao, who set up so many dates for you.'

'I don't hate her. I simply dislike her. She'd match me off with anyone as long as it would get her husband promoted.'

'See, Mei, this is your problem. You don't trust anyone. People try to help you, but you always think they have ulterior motives. Perhaps they do, perhaps they don't – what does it matter?'

'It matters a lot. It matters whether people are truthful.'

'You are my older sister, but you can be so naïve sometimes. No wonder you have many enemies.'

'Would you rather that I don't come to your wedding? That would save the embarrassment for everyone.'

'Of course I want you there. You are my sister, my family. How can you even think like this?' Lu paused for a minute. The temperature between them cooled a few degrees. 'Mei, I admire your high standards. But other people are not as noble as you. You pass judgment on them. Sometimes I wish you could be just a bit more tolerant.'

That night, alone in her apartment, Mei watched the yellow and red lightshow on the ring-road below her window. She thought about her shortcomings. She too wished that she were more tolerant. She wondered whether those so-called high standards were the cause of her sorry state – all alone and out of a job. Perhaps Lu was right. Who was she to judge other people?

Then she tried to imagine what the world would be like if people spoke their minds. In such a world, Lu would have told

Mei that she did not fit in with her sister's perfect image and Mei would have understood, as she did now. Face and image were everything to Lu. In that world, no one would stop Mei from telling Mrs Yao that she was not a stepping stone for her husband's career and that her happiness was not to be traded like a favour.

Mei thought about not going to the wedding, and how shocked and angry everyone would be. She knew that it was never a real possibility, but she played the scenario in her head: a meditation of protest.

In the end, she did go to the wedding, as she knew she had to.

The legal procedures – permission from the Party (Lining had the blessing of the Mayor, of course), medical examinations and the marriage certificate with a joint portrait – had all been completed. The only thing remaining was a grand reception.

The day turned out to be perfect. Ocean-blue sky spread out to eternity. When sunshine hit the skin, it bestowed an intimate warmth like the touch of a loved one. The tops of the French oak trees lining the street stirred in a feather-like breeze, radiating dappled light in all directions. The air was as clear as filtered water.

Two hundred and eighty-six red lanterns dangled from the butterfly roof of the restaurant. Two more enormous lanterns hung by the entrance like a pair of earrings, flashing the words Double Happiness. Thirty parking attendants in red mandarin-collared shirts and wide trousers buzzed about like a horde of beetles ferrying Mercedes and Audis to the front of the parking lot and cars like Mei's red Mitsubishi to the back. They were young migrant workers, fit as oxen and always prepared to work sixteen hours a day.

At the door, a four-man team had been setting off belts of firecrackers since the first guest arrived. The air reeked of gunpowder and smoke.

'How many times have I told you? Get to the side, too much smoke!' one of the wedding organisers shouted at the firecracker crew.

The organiser was a chubby woman in her late thirties, who wore a pink silk skirt suit with a red flower pinned just above her large breasts. Whenever she smiled, which was almost constantly, she flashed a full set of blinding white teeth. She greeted Mei with a Buddha bow, palms together under her chin. Mei wondered whether anyone had thought about wrapping her up in red ribbons.

Once Mei had passed through the firecrackers and the smoke, the scene inside the restaurant was graceful and orderly. A red carpet ran from the entrance to a two-metre-high stage at the back. On each side of the red carpet were rows of chairs that could be taken away after the ceremony. It looked as if all the guests had arrived. There wasn't a single empty chair in sight.

Near the stage were sixteen ten-person tables seating eight on each side, for the bride and groom's families and the most distinguished guests. One of the eighty-eight waitresses in figure-hugging *Qi Pao* dresses showed Mei to the Wang family table. A pink lotus flower floated in a crystal vase placed at the table's centre. It must have been picked early that morning, for it looked as fresh as morning dew. Scattered on the table were red rose petals.

Little Auntie had arrived from Shanghai. She was Mama's baby sister, twelve years younger than Ling Bai. Sitting next to Little Auntie was her sixteen-year-old son with a face full of pimples. He was talking to Uncle Chen's daughter, who wore a frozen smile. *Someone get me out of here*, her eyes pleaded. Her older brother, born in the same year as Lu, was fending off his mother, Auntie Chen, with nothing more than a *yes* or *no* in a verbal ping-pong match. But the mother always smashed back. It was going to be a long day.

'You're late,' whispered Mama before Mei could sit down.

'The wedding's not going to start for another ten minutes.' Mei took up her assigned position.

'You are family, you've got responsibilities. Many guests have come over to offer their congratulations and I am here all alone.'

'Sorry.'

Mei said a quick hello to Uncle Chen, who was seated next to her. Uncle Chen was not really Mei's uncle, but Mama's best friend. He and Mama had known each other since they were at high school in Shanghai. When the children were young, the two families used to go on outings together and visited each other for Chinese New Year. After Mei's father died, Uncle Chen continued to visit, but mostly without his family.

'Now, quickly go and say hello to Lining's family,' urged Mama.

'All right,' Mei grunted, and got up from her seat.

She crossed the red dividing line and greeted Lining's family. She had already met them on various occasions: his parents, younger brother, sister-in-law and two nephews, who lived in Vancouver, and his much younger sister and her American boyfriend, who were studying film at UCLA. Lining had grown up in Dalai, the northern industrial centre considered the shipyard of China. His father was the head of a small machine tool factory and his mother was a nurse. Lining had first made it big through oil refineries, before moving into shipping and real estate. He had bought a house in Vancouver for his parents. His brother was his North American representative.

'Come over, Mei, let me look at you.' Lining's mother, Mrs Jiang, extended her hand for Mei to take.

'Every time I see you and Lu, I say to your mother, how prosperous, two beautiful *Qian Jin*, a thousand gold pieces!' Mrs Jiang exclaimed in her usual state of excitement. 'You are worth ten thousand gold pieces. So I tell her.'

'Auntie Jiang is exaggerating,' said Mei, an answer straight from the social etiquette handbook. After all, she was not entirely without polish.

'I don't understand how you can still be single,' said Mrs Jiang, sounding almost angry. 'My child, sometimes one can set one's bar too high. If you like, give Auntie Jiang a word, I will find you a nice husband in Vancouver.'

Mr Jiang senior interrupted his wife. 'Stop bugging the child about it. You do it all the time. Let her live her own life.' He turned to Mei and asked, 'I hear that you have left the Ministry for Public Security. What are you going to do?'

'I am going to be a private detective,' Mei answered. To her surprise she found her voice shrinking. She thought she'd come to the wedding with her head held high. She thought she'd be proud of her new life. Instead, she was embarrassed.

'Really?' cried Lining's little sister. 'How exciting. Are you the first private eye in Beijing? Do you have murder cases?'

Mei was just about to answer both questions in the negative when a big guy in a dark suit and trendy brown leather tie jumped out from nowhere. 'Congratulations!' he shouted.

'Ah, Mr Hu. Happy together!' Lining's brother greeted him in the same way. He explained to his father, 'Mr Hu is the Party Chairman at Beijing Second Factory for Firecrackers and Gunpowder.'

'Do you like the firecrackers?' asked the Party man, who

apparently needed no answer in order to carry on. 'They're our best bangers, those little bastards. I told Lining, no worries, leave it to me. I've got another truckload of them in the parking lot.'

'Is it safe?' asked Mr Jiang senior.

'What do you mean?'

'Well, leaving a truck of explosives outside on such a dry sunny day.'

'No problem. Got two kids sitting on them,' said Mr Hu, unconcerned.

Mei seized the opportunity to take her leave. As soon as she sat down, a grave young pianist in tails struck the first note of the wedding march. The groom and best man emerged from behind the giant Double Happiness banner. Slowly, the bridesmaids, little angels in rose dresses, walked down the red carpet. Behind them, on the arm of the Deputy Mayor of Beijing, Lu looked like a goddess travelling on sweeping white clouds.

The bride and the groom appeared perfectly suited, despite the fifteen-year age gap. Lining was of middling height with a well-toned body. He had the confident air of an extremely successful man. He looked much younger than his age. Lu, on the other hand, was more elegant and sophisticated than the average twenty-six-year-old. As for their personalities, Mei thought that they had much in common.

Mei remembered when Lu first met Lining. She had said that she did not like him – he was too old, he was divorced, he was arrogant. He was someone who had too many girls throwing themselves at him, someone used to getting everything he wanted. Mei wondered whether Lu actually felt like that or if it was the kind of talk intended to make Lining chase her harder.

After the Western wedding ceremony, the bride and groom went away to change. The pop star Tian Tian sprang onto the stage, rocking his hips and singing his latest hits. They were all about love and devotion. Misty-eyed young women swooned in ecstasy. Mei hummed along wordlessly. She was happy, she was enjoying the party, and like everyone else she was impressed by the exclusiveness.

Twenty minutes later, Tian Tian yielded the floor to the chubby lady in the pink suit. The groom was now dressed in a long midnight-blue silk robe with golden embroidery. The bride wore a red Chinese wedding gown and jewelled cape.

'Bow to heaven!' shouted shark's teeth, her voice unexpectedly loud.

The bride and groom bowed north, at the Double Happiness banner.

'Bow to earth!'

They turned and bowed south.

'Bow to parents!'

They did as they were told.

'Husband and wife, bow to each other!'

The groom lifted the bride's red veil.

The crowd roared. 'Eat dried plums!' they shouted. 'Eat peanuts!'

Lu blushed like a sweet young girl of eighteen. The guests shouted again, '*Zao Sheng Zi*! Dried plums and raw peanuts!' These symbolised the guests' wish that the newlyweds be blessed with sons before long.

Outside, a battery of firecrackers burst again.

For a second time, the couple went away to change. The grand piano was once more pushed onto the stage. Graceful waitresses in tight *Qi Pao* ushered guests upstairs to their tables. The manager and floor managers shouted. Young migrant help-hands stacked the chairs and carried them out. Two large rosewood tables were brought in. A big crystal bowl filled with Red Pockets stuffed with cash was placed on one of them and, on the other, assortments of gifts of various colours, shapes and sizes.

Cigarettes were lit, the smoke from them rising and filling the room. When everyone was seated, the banquet was served: a sumptuous array of cold cuts, bird's nest soup, marinated seahorse, jellyfish, crabmeat in coconut shells, fish carved into the shape of squirrels, spicy seafood hot pots and jade green vegetables.

Uncle Chen leaned over and said to Mama, 'Such great food and a lovely wedding too.'

'It has come out nicely, hasn't it?' Mama glowed. 'So many people have come to honour the occasion – the Deputy Mayor and all the big bosses, your family, Lining's family coming from Canada. Lu's done well.'

'They do say, "better lucky than able". Lu is an exceptional girl: beautiful, smart and successful in her own right. But she *is* a lucky girl to have married so well!' Uncle Chen grinned.

Mama beamed too.

'Let's drink to Lu's luck and Old Ling's luck!' Uncle Chen stood up and raised his rice wine.

'Lucky!' shouted everyone at the table, raising their glasses.

'Lucky, lucky.' Mama bowed with a wide smile and emptied the rice wine in her shot cup.

Uncle Chen sat down again. 'You must be so proud of her,' he laughed. 'Now you can sit back and enjoy your good fortune.'

'I wish I could,' sighed Mama. 'Let me say this today: I've never had to worry about Lu. That child has always been sensible, good with people. Our ancestors say the two aims in life are to "make a family and build a career". Now she's done both.'

Uncle Chen nodded his agreement. Shredded cold lobster had arrived, and he was too busy eating to speak.

Mei decided to ignore Mama, though she understood that her mother was saying these words for her benefit. Mei wasn't interested in *Guanxi*. She believed in herself. She believed that as long as she was capable, she would succeed.

The newlyweds reappeared. Lu had changed into a white trouser suit, her hair swept back in a bun, showing off a pair of sparkling diamond earrings. She walked with her new husband, now in a smart dark suit, toasting the distinguished guests. Lu, who normally drank little, worked the floor with a glass of champagne in hand. Lining happily followed with a cup of lethal Chinese rice wine. Mei knew that after this round Lu would change her outfit again before continuing their journey upstairs, paying respect to all the guests.

'Are you okay?' Uncle Chen seemed to notice Mei's long face.

Mei shrugged and tried to smile. 'Fine.'

'It can't be easy to be the unmarried older sister,' said Uncle Chen.

From everywhere, Mei heard loud voices, people laughing, singing and drinking; bowls, chopsticks and plates clattering. There were sweaty faces, cigarette smoke and the smell of rice wine. Some eyes met Mei's with inquisitive stares. They smiled, nodding knowingly.

'Don't let it bother you,' Mei heard Uncle Chen saying.

'I'm fine. I don't really care,' she lied.

'You can't stop people talking. Some people feed on this stuff. They gossip and judge others so that they can feel superior. But I'll tell you something,' Uncle Chen whispered, 'you've always been my favourite. I'm not saying that I don't like Lu, but I think you're different. You're brave. You don't chase things like everyone else. Lu's happy now, but for how long? Soon there'll be another thing she wants and then another.'

'Well, at least she is married,' Mei frowned.

Uncle Chen tapped her shoulder. 'You will be too.'

Presently, a well-dressed tallish woman in her fifties approached them tentatively, lowering her head to get a better look at Uncle Chen.

'Old Chen, I thought it was you!'

Immediately she extended her right hand. 'I was sitting over there and thought that man looked a lot like Chen Jitian.'

Uncle Chen stared first at the woman's round face and then at her small white hand, his mouth half-open as if waiting for words to rise from his guts. He tried to get up. In a violent jolt, his chair flipped, slapping his tummy on the edge of the table. But he bounced back to grab her hand, his eyes smiling. 'Xiao Qing, what a surprise. How are you? How long has it been since we last saw each other?'

'Our university's thirtieth anniversary in 1984. How are you doing? Still working at Xinhua News Agency?'

Ms Qing stood at the same height as Uncle Chen, but in contrast to his plumpness and receding hairline she was slender and sported a fashionable perm.

'Yes, the same old.' Uncle Chen kept smiling.

'Good. Give me a call next week; let's get together.' Ms Qing handed him a business card. The newlyweds had arrived at her table. She had to go.

'Sure thing.' Uncle Chen nodded like a rooster.

Ms Qing had already turned around and walked away.

What was left of the seafood dishes was removed to make space for a large suckling duck, carved and re-laid over a bed of Chinese cabbage. Uncle Chen picked up a paper-thin pancake and covered it in sweet wheat sauce, two slices of the best duck meat and a few slivers of spring onions. He rolled it up for Mei.

'Thank you, but I am so full,' said Mei, looking at the nicest thing someone had done for her all day.

'Must eat. Food is one of the great pleasures in life,' Uncle Chen insisted, pushing the plate closer to Mei.

Mei smiled and took a bite. She noticed that Uncle Chen had not touched the duck at all.

'Who was that?' asked Mei, pointing her chin at Ms Qing's table.

'Oh, someone I knew from university,' said Uncle Chen. 'She was a year behind me. But look at what she is doing now!' He slid the business card over.

Ms Yun Qing, Chairwoman, Beijing Jeep, a Joint Venture with Chrysler.

'Mei, let me tell you something. You are doing the right thing starting your own business. This is the time to do it, to take charge of your life. Don't wait till it's too late.'

'Too late?'

'Look at me. I always followed the orders of the Party, did my duty and waited all my life to be noticed. I will be sixty next year and soon I will retire. What have I got? Stuck in no-hope land. Too late.'

Mei had never seen Uncle Chen unhappy like this. She thought that perhaps he had had too much to drink.

She looked again at the crowd of people eating, drinking and talking. Firecrackers exploded outside. Mei felt trapped, as if she and everyone around her were locked inside a city under siege. Those who were outside wanted to get in and those who were inside wanted to get out.

7

Over eighteen months had passed since Lu's wedding, and, if anything, Uncle Chen seemed to have grown even rounder.

'You must be wondering why I am here.' Uncle Chen struggled to settle his wide body into the sofa chair. He was smiling, but seemed embarrassed and awkward. 'Oh, these cookies are good. "Product of Belgium", I see.'

Eating seemed to calm him. His smiles became more genuine and he shifted in the chair with less effort.

Gupin brewed Oolong tea in a cast-iron pot. Mei poured two cups, one for Uncle Chen and one for herself.

Uncle Chen whispered, 'Your assistant is a man? And he makes tea for you?'

'Yes,' Mei said perkily. She was used to people asking such questions, as though there was something bizarre about her or Gupin. Some of them no doubt suspected her of being a menacing boss, a dragon lady. As for Gupin, they may have had worse suspicions.

'Where is he from? He has an accent.'

'Henan. He is a migrant worker. But he has a high school diploma. He is streetwise as well as kind. His mother is paralysed. He sends money home.'

Mei stopped. She realised that she was trying to justify hiring Gupin.

'He seems nice.' Uncle Chen nodded politely.

They quickly moved off the subject of Gupin.

'Where should I start?' Uncle Chen said. 'I suppose I should start from the beginning.' He leaned back in his seat. 'It was the winter of 1968. I had been working for the Xinhua News Agency for four years. I had just turned thirty. Hard to believe?' Uncle Chen waved a cookie like a flag and laughed from his stomach in the way chubby men do. 'Yes, I was your age once.'

Mei smiled back. It was good to see an old friend. Uncle Chen, round and kind-looking, had the air about him of a smiling Buddha.

'It was a harsh winter, a lot of snow and chaos and bloodshed. The Red Guard were fighting amongst themselves, each faction claiming to be the most loyal and true representative of Maoism. They set up barricades inside universities, factories and government compounds, and bombarded each other with machine guns. Well, you know all about that.'

But Mei wasn't listening. Uncle Chen's voice had travelled through her ears like wind through a hollow tree. Instead, she was looking at Uncle Chen closely. Age had taken away his hair the way summer laid claim to the harvest. Mei could see the dye. It was not expensive. It had dried out his head, giving it the look of parched earth.

'Today everyone knows about all that. But back then the Central Government did not know the extent of what was happening on the ground. The Red Guard and Youth Party members had smashed all the normal communications systems. So the Agency sent me to Luoyang to report on the goings-on there.'

'Why Luoyang?' Mei took a sip of her tea, returning her attention to Uncle Chen's story.

'Someone had to go to Luoyang and it turned out to be me. Did you know that Luoyang was the last capital of the Han Dynasty? Anyway, the situation there was no different from the rest of the country. The Red Guard had ransacked everything, including the Luoyang Museum. After they destroyed the relics, they piled up the paintings, documents and records and set the museum on fire. So, naturally, people assumed that everything the museum had went up in the flames.'

Mei refilled the teacup for Uncle Chen.

'Thanks. Two days ago, a ceremonial bowl that was once part of the Luoyang Museum collection turned up in Hong Kong. Now you understand where I am going with this, don't you? Yes. If the bowl survived, other pieces might have too.'

'You mean someone took them before the museum was burned down?'

'Someone stole them!' snapped Uncle Chen. 'And the Luoyang Museum had one very special piece indeed. Only a few people from the museum knew about it, and as far as I know they were either killed by the Red Guard or later died in labour camps. Would you like to hear the story?'

Uncle Chen had now made himself at home. He reached for another cookie.

'Emperor Xian was the last Emperor of Han. He was only fifteen years old when the rebel force arrived in Chang'an in 194 AD. The royal army had fought the rebels for weeks. It was losing the battle. Realising that the West Gate could no longer be defended, Emperor Xian gathered together his advisors at the palace. The counsellors recommended evacuation of the capital. But one person came forth to oppose the idea, saying that they would bring shame on their ancestors and the founding emperor Gao Zu if they gave up Chang'an. He offered to lead the Imperial Guards to combat. This man was General Cao Cao.'

'King Cao Cao of the Three Kingdoms?'

'Yes, the future ruler of China. So Cao Cao went back to the Cao compound to get ready for battle. Like everyone else, he knew that he might not live to see another day. After all, there were only eight thousand Imperial Guards, though they were the best and the bravest, and the rebel force was twenty thousand strong.

'Before leaving for battle, Cao Cao wrote two letters. One of these he gave to his housekeeper to deliver to his wife, Ding, in Ann Hui. Back then, if you were a rich aristocrat, you could have many wives and concubines. But there was always the joint-heir wife, who was the head wife. Ding was Cao Cao's joint-heir wife. The other letter he wrote was for Lady Cai Wenji.'

'The famous poet!' Mei exclaimed.

'Yes. Cao Cao asked one of his most trusted captains to escort Lady Cai from Chang'an back to her hometown. Then he untied the sash from his waist and gave it to the captain together with the letter.'

The cookies had vanished. Uncle Chen was growing more animated.

'The captain and his men galloped to the Cai residence. Chang'an was in chaos. One million inhabitants plus tens of thousands of refugees who had fled into the city ahead of the rebel forces were moving out. They went on foot, on horses, in carriages and on wooden carts. At the Cai compound, Lady Cai read the letter. She hid the sash in her wide sleeve and ordered that the letter be burned. Lady Cai was later captured by the rebels and sold to the King of South Mongolia. She lived in the Mongolian grassland for the next twelve years, bore the Mongol King two children, and wrote her most celebrated poems about her longing to return to China.

'Against all odds, Cao Cao defeated the rebel forces and saved the ancient city of Chang'an. But he couldn't save the Han Dynasty, which soon disintegrated into three kingdoms. When he was crowned the King of Kingdom Wei, he discovered that Lady Cai was alive and living in Mongolia. He sent a representative there with one million gold pieces to buy her freedom. The Mongol King agreed to let Lady Cai leave, but not her children. Lady Cai chose to come home.'

'I can't believe she would leave her children behind,' said Mei.

'People do amazing things for love.' Uncle Chen raised his eyebrows.

'You mean Lady Cai and Cao Cao were lovers?'

Uncle Chen nodded. 'The key to a legend that is over one thousand years old has brought me here. Now can you guess what was in the Luoyang Museum?'

'The sash?'

'Clever girl. Almost. The museum had in its possession what was inside the sash – Cao Cao's jade seal. In the Han Dynasty, officials carried their seals in sashes tied to their waists. They wore long colourful ribbons around their waists to show their rank. For example, the prime minister's ribbon was red and two *zhang* long.'

Watching Uncle Chen take a long draught of his Oolong tea, Mei wondered what his connection with the treasure was and why he had come to see her about it. She knew that Uncle Chen loved art, but something this valuable was surely out of his league.

Uncle Chen leaned forward, lowering his voice. 'I would like you to find the jade seal.'

'But something like that must be a national treasure.' Mei frowned. National treasures belonged to the country and were not allowed to be traded by individuals.

'Precisely.' Uncle Chen clapped his hands. 'This is why I don't want to use reporters and certainly not the police. One wrong step, and the jade would be on its way to Hong Kong before you know it.'

Mei did not move or say a word. Instead she watched Uncle Chen, her eyes deep as mountain lakes.

'Don't worry. I am not asking you to do anything illegal. A Chinese collector I know is willing to pay a lot of money for the jade, all hard US dollars, to keep it inside China.' He sat back, sinking into the chair, and smiled. 'Would Uncle Chen put you in harm's way? Everything is above board, I've checked. You trust me, don't you?'

'Of course,' said Mei, embarrassed.

'That's good.' Uncle Chen nodded. He pushed himself up from the pit of the sofa chair, and took out a neatly folded piece of paper. It was a cutting from a newspaper.

'Start with Pu Yan,' said Uncle Chen. 'He works at the Research Institute for Cultural Relics. He has a private gig on the side – an antique consultancy, you could call it. From time to time, he does valuations and authentication work for dealers. If you go see him, he will be able to put you on the right track.'

'How much should I tell him?'

'Pu Yan is an old friend. You can be honest with him.'

Uncle Chen moved towards the door.

'Remember when you first opened this agency, I said that you were doing the right thing? You are, my child. You will one day have both fame and fortune.' Uncle Chen beamed, nodding as if to congratulate himself on his foresight.

'I will go see your mother one of these days,' said Uncle Chen, turning the door knob. 'But I'd rather that you don't tell her about our little meeting today.'

8

After dinner, Mei called Pu Yan.

'Yes, Old Chen told me you'd call.' A soft and slightly accented voice came through the receiver. 'You are looking for a jade from the Han Dynasty? No, there are none left.'

'If you could give me a pointer or two and perhaps tell me where to go and how to look . . .'

'I'd be happy to answer your questions. But if you would allow me to give you a word from my heart, you are going on a wild-goose chase,' said Pu Yan in his sing-song voice.

Mei smiled. 'When is a good time to meet?'

'When are you thinking of?'

'The sooner the better.'

'Well, the weather's terrible.'

Mei looked outside and agreed.

'There's an ice rink inside China World,' Pu Yan said. 'Do you know where it is? Good. We can meet there tomorrow evening at six o'clock.'

'How will I find you?'

'Look for me in the café by the rink. I'm old. Fifty-seven.'

Mei wondered what to do with such a description.

'You won't have any trouble spotting me,' said Pu Yan, as if he could read her mind. 'There's hardly anyone over thirty-five there.'

'In case I can't find you,' Mei said, 'I am thirty years old, with a round face and shoulder-length hair. My nose is a bit sharp. People say it makes me look angry. I will wear a red woollen hat.'

The café was full when Mei arrived. The chairs by the glass partition had been turned around so that people could watch the ice-skaters. A group of businessmen in dark suits were having an argument with the head waiter and an upset-looking waitress. Two Western men chatted quietly at a corner table. A group of youths stared at Mei when she walked in to the café. It had to be the hat, thought Mei; she felt as if she were a red-crowned rooster on parade. She looked round for Pu Yan but saw no one older than thirty-five, as he had warned her.

Mei looked at her watch. It showed five minutes past six. She found a small table and sat down to watch the skaters.

The ice was white, like a delicious candy. A girl, perhaps ten years old, skated in a pink costume in the middle of the rink. One moment she set off flying like a magpie and a minute later she was spinning like a long-necked swan. Though she pretended not to notice the gaze of onlookers, it was clear that she loved to dazzle and she performed as if she were skating in an Olympic competition.

Mei blinked. The lights were too bright. They made her eyes ache.

A waiter arrived. Mei ordered Oolong tea and surveyed the room again. She saw only youth and happiness.

'Are you Miss Wang?'

Mei turned around. She could swear that there hadn't been anyone standing there when she checked two minutes earlier.

'I am Pu Yan,' said the man. He was short and stocky and carried a holdall.

Mei stood up. 'How do you do.'

Pu Yan looked younger than she had expected. He had soft southern features – smooth curves around his mouth, vulnerable thin lips. He wore a number of layers under his open coat: a dark jacket, a grey knitted vest, a brown sweater and a button-down shirt. They were typical state-run department store finds, not fashionable, but thoughtfully put together. When he spoke, his facial features seemed to soften even further. Mei liked him straight away.

He sat down across the table from her and pointed at the ice rink. 'I saw you from out there. You see the little girl in pink? That's my granddaughter. Isn't she magnificent? She is already at the city junior level. Such a fancy place to skate, though; she just loves the attention.'

Mei smiled. 'Does she come here often?'

'Oh, goodness no. She normally trains at the City Children's Sports Hall. Look how happy she is on that ice! Poor girl, her parents are divorced. Her father went to England. She hardly sees her mother because my daughter works very hard in a Hong Kong advertising firm. She makes good money, though, so from time to time we bring her here for a treat. We live nearby, in the Central Arts and Crafts College, just the other side of the ring-road. My wife teaches there.'

Mei looked again and saw the girl flying across the ice like a vision in pink.

The waiter brought them tea. Mei asked for some preserved plums and roasted sunflower seeds.

'Do you know much about jade?' Pu Yan asked her.

Mei shook her head.

'Westerners always like green jade. The Mayas used to use jade as a weapon because it's a strong stone, stronger than steel. But in China white jade is more valuable; it's called the Stone of Heaven. Have you heard of Hetian White Jade?' Pu Yan reached under the table and produced two small white cardboard boxes from his holdall.

'Hetian is a remote outpost at the bottom of the Taklamakan Desert in Xinjiang province. Hetian White Jade comes from the deposit by the banks of Jade Dragon Kashgar River. White jade is quite rare now, because after thousands of years of mining, the deposit is exhausted.'

The waiter brought the snacks and poured tea for both of them.

Pu Yan opened the boxes and handed Mei two small pieces of jade. They were each the size of a business card, and about two centimetres thick. When Mei held them in her hands, she could feel the coolness of the stone. They were creamy white and smooth, and seemed to glow with clarity. One of the pieces was decorated with delicate carvings of clouds and natural scenery and the other was inscribed with a lady in traditional attire.

'Look at them under the light,' Pu Yan said. 'Look at the smoothness and transparency of the jade, and then look at the carvings. Jade is a very hard material, difficult to work with. But look at how detailed these carvings are.'

'Are these new?' Mei rubbed the pieces of jade in her hands. They felt pure.

'Unfortunately, they are. Today it's almost impossible to find antique Hetian White Jade pieces. A lot of them were destroyed in the Cultural Revolution. If even one piece had been sold on the market it would have fetched a fortune. Even the new ones are expensive; these cost a few thousand yuan each.'

Pu Yan gestured for Mei to give back the jade. 'I have to return them to the research institute tomorrow,' he said casually, putting the pieces back in their boxes. 'Tell me about the jade you are looking for. It's from the Han Dynasty, you say?'

Mei told him that the jade was believed to be a seal that had belonged to Cao Cao.

'That would be something, wouldn't it?' Pu Yan exclaimed.

Mei repeated the story Uncle Chen had told her and showed Pu Yan the newspaper article Uncle Chen had given her about the ceremonial bowl.

Pu Yan studied the picture of the bowl. It was a rustic brown ceramic decorated with paintings of galloping horses and battle scenes. He then read the article. Mei drank her tea and ate the dried plums. Outside, the loudspeaker boomed out the Carpenters' 'Yesterday Once More'.

'Sold for sixty thousand US dollars!' Pu Yan muttered to himself. 'That would be more than half a million yuan!' He nodded as if taking a mental note. 'I have heard about this ceremonial bowl. You see, sometimes I do antique valuations. We valuers belong to a small circle.' He handed the newspaper cutting back to Mei. 'I believe the bowl was sold to one of the dealers in Liulichang. I suppose either the dealer or someone associated with him smuggled it to Hong Kong. Trading and exporting national treasures is a crime punishable with thirty years in jail. But people still do it, for money.'

'How much do you think the dealer originally paid for it?'

'I'd say perhaps thirty-five to forty thousand yuan. That's a lot of money for a Chinese person, especially when the seller is from the provinces.'

'Do you know which dealer bought the bowl?'

'No. But you may be able to find out. It won't be easy to get people to talk, but everything has a price – especially these days. Ah!' Pu Yan's eyes lit up. He waved his right hand. 'Here comes my granddaughter.'

Mei turned around. The girl in pink approached carefully. Her cheeks were flushed with warmth from skating. Her flat chest moved rapidly up and down. As soon as she saw her grandfather's extended arms, she ran to him, her skinny ponytail flapping behind her.

'Hong Hong, this is Miss Wang, the lady I told you about.'

Hong Hong looked at Mei with her big eyes.

'Would you like some coconut milk?' Pu Yan whispered into his granddaughter's ear. The ponytail nodded.

Pu Yan waved at a passing waitress for the drink and asked Hong Hong to sit next to him.

'How do you know Old Chen?' Pu Yan asked, relaxing in his chair.

'Uncle Chen is an old friend of my mother's. They went to the same high school in Shanghai,' said Mei. 'Where do you know Uncle Chen from?'

'Did he not tell you?'

'No.'

Pu Yan sat up and pushed his teacup to the side. Mei had a feeling that he was going to tell her a long story. People of Uncle Chen and her mother's generation loved talking about the past.

'Chen Jitian and I met through sheep,' said Pu Yan earnestly.

'Sheep?'

'Have you been to Inner Mongolia?'

'No,' said Mei. 'But one day I'd like to go there.'

'You should. It's a beautiful place, in some ways a bare place, good for the soul. I was there during the Cultural Revolution. We were called smelly intellectuals back then. Chairman Mao said we needed reform, so we were sent to labour camps to work with our hands and feet.

'Before I went there, I thought of Inner Mongolia as lush grassland dotted with white sheep under blue sky. I imagined lazy summer days filled with the scents of lavender and dandelions. How wrong I was. Life wasn't like that at all. Most of Inner Mongolia is desert, the Gobi Desert.

'Winters were long and harsh; summers were hot and short. There were sandstorms in spring and autumn. To make things worse, we had a diet that consisted of only one ingredient – mutton: braised, boiled, roasted or cooked whichever way. Whenever you walked into the canteen, the smell hit you.

'One thing I did like was herding sheep. I liked to take them to a good feed. I liked to be alone with the vastness of that wonderland. Most of all, I enjoyed being far away from the camp, far away from being bothered. I had this old smelly dog called Not Yet Dead that liked nothing better than lying at my feet and farting. I liked him too.

'One day, I decided to explore a new steppe that someone had told me about. I got there at noon. The sun was shining. Clouds moved like train engines across the sky. I let the sheep loose and lay down on the grass.

'Do you know how it felt to be there? It felt like being lost at sea. The wild landscape extended as far as the eyes could see. It was easy to forget who you were in that overwhelming vastness. The land had such a power. It could make you lose your sense of self and make you feel as though you were a drop of water melting away in what was merely an illusion of life.

'I think I must have gone to sleep after a while, because when I woke up, the sky was dark. The wind had picked up, swaying the long grass. I kicked my useless dog and we started to gather the sheep together to go back. But not long after we started off, a sandstorm caught us. Soon we couldn't see where we were going.

'Somewhere along the way, not exactly going back to the camp as it turned out, we ran into another herd of sheep. The two herds got mixed up. The other herd had two shepherds, one very young, almost a boy, and the other a stout man who was confused and out of his wits. So we all shouted and tried to pull our herds apart, trying to move on, where to I had no idea. Not Yet Dead jumped up and down, barking.

'But we couldn't do it, so eventually we herded all the sheep in the same direction. It was a miracle that we ended up back at my camp. I remember all these people running out to help us. Many of them had been watching and waiting for a long time.

'After the sheep had been locked up, I invited the two shepherds to my dorm for tea. The chubby one was Chen Jitian. It turned out that the Xinhua News Agency had a labour camp not far from ours.

'From then on, Old Chen and I frequently met up with our sheep. We shared food and chatted about life. Out there on the grassland, we had a lot of time, and we talked about all kinds of things. Sometimes we read Mao's *Little Red Book*, the only book we had with us. Sometimes we talked about history or art or relics.

'At the time we were both frustrated with life, as almost everyone was. But I could sense that the kind of frustration was somehow deeper with Lao Chen. Yet because he was so nice, so agreeable and mild-tempered, his complaints were like a whimper compared to mine. The Chens moved back to Beijing a year before we did. But we kept in touch.'

'Do you still see him and his family?'

'Not as much as I'd like to. We are all so busy these days. I was glad to hear that he is finally a senior editor. He'd wanted it for a long time. I was happy, too, when he called. I used to help him a lot with his herds – he was probably the worst shepherd in the steppe, and in the two years I knew him he never improved.'

Hong Hong looked tired. Mei waved the waiter over and asked for the bill.

'Would you like a ride home?' Mei ask Pu Yan. 'I've got a car.'

'Whoa, you must do pretty well!' exclaimed Pu Yan. Then he said in his sing-song voice, 'No, thank you. From here the underground path leads directly to the subway station.' He took Hong Hong's hand. 'We will be home before long.'

9

There is never a clearer spring day than the one after a yellow sandstorm. That morning the sky was as blue and infinite as the virgin sea. The air was brisk, filled with watery particles of the morning mist now soaking up warm sunshine.

Mei wore a pea-green coat belted over a black turtleneck sweater and black trousers. Her hair was pinned up in a French twist. A fake gold-chained Chanel bag she had bought at the Silk Market dangled from her shoulder as she walked, high heels clicking. She looked like someone with money, the only type of person who could afford to shop in Liulichang.

Liulichang, the oldest shopping area in Beijing, was famous throughout China for works of art and antiques. A short distance from Tiananmen Square, outside Peace Gate, Liulichang flourished during the Ming Dynasty, when the emperor banned shops and theatres within the city walls.

Mei remembered coming with her mother to the western half of Liulichang – the part that dealt with ancient books, calligraphy and traditional Chinese ink painting – to buy ink stone and rubbings and to have Mama's paintings mounted on scrolls. It was on one of these trips that her mother bought her a seal and had her name engraved on it by the craftsman at *Rongbaozhai*, the Studio of Glorious Treasures. But they had not been here in recent years. Liulichang was now frequented mostly by foreign tourists and the rich.

The antique market ran along the eastern half of the street. It had been rebuilt in the 1980s in the style of the previous century: two-storey mansions with grey butterfly roofs and burgundy windowpanes. Mei eliminated state-owned shops from her search, as well as the bazaar types rented by small vendors. Only the big privately owned shops could afford to buy and sell something as expensive as the Han ceremonial bowl.

There was one such shop on the north side of the street. It had a wide front room lined with glass cabinets of ink stones, jade and coral ornaments. Mei's first instinct was that it might just be the kind of place the seller of the Han Dynasty bowl could have stopped at. But once she walked into the back room, she was disappointed to find it packed with Chinese ink paintings.

On the wall a large poster advertised a painter whose work was prominently displayed in the room. The artist was a National Second Grade painter and a member of the Chinese Painting Academy. The room itself was taken up by two large wooden tables piled with rolls of paper, colour, ink and brushes. A man dressed neatly in a tailor-made Mao jacket – and who bore a noticeable resemblance to the artist in the poster – sat on a long bench.

When Mei asked, the man said he was indeed the artist, and he could paint anything on request. 'How about a phoenix like this?' He pointed at one of his paintings hanging on the wall. 'Or red plum bloom in snow, perhaps?'

Mei declined, thanking the artist, and left. She felt irritated that she had disappointed him. He reminded her of her mother. Ling Bai painted traditional Chinese ink paintings too. She always said that her paintings weren't very good, but Mei loved them, and had filled her apartment with her mother's pictures.

Mei crossed the street and entered a shop on the ground floor of a grand mansion. The shop stocked all kinds of goods, from medicine cabinets, wooden pillows, brides' chests and bronze Buddhas to opium pipes, stone tablets and jade. Things seemed to be organised by size and height: large pieces were stacked up by the back wall, while smaller items were displayed within reach of the shopkeeper's hands. The room was dark. To compensate, there were a few traditional silk lamps, casting shadows.

'Hello, miss, looking for something specific?' Mei heard a crisp voice coming from behind her.

She turned around and saw a boy with smiling eyes.

'Whatever you like, I can give you a really good price.' The boy came closer.

'Is the boss here?' Mei asked. 'I'd like a word.'

The boy was disappointed. His smile shrank a little. 'Uncle, someone wants to see you!' he hollered.

Part of the black shadow that had covered most of the back wall broke off. It began to change shape. The light from the window drew out a profile – a flat nose, small eyes, age-spots and wrinkles that looked like fine cuts. It was an ordinary face, easily missed. The old man wore a black Tang jacket and a pair of black wide trousers, giving the illusion that he could walk through shadows. He peered about him, moving as quietly as night.

'This little sister wants to talk to you!' the boy yelled.

When he reached her, Mei saw that the old man was a fraction shorter than she was.

'I am disturbing you.' Mei took out a picture of the ceremonial bowl. 'But I want to ask whether you have seen this?'

'You need to speak up, my uncle doesn't hear too well,' the boy said. He shouted to the old man: 'The little sister asks whether you've seen this bowl!'

The old man studied the picture, holding it inches from his eyes. He stared at it with such concentration he could have been looking for some invisible code. 'You a police?' he asked, rolling his tongue at the end of the sentence, the old Beijing way.

'No. I'm a collector!' Mei shouted.

The old man stared into her face the same way he had looked at the picture. Mei looked straight back at him, trying to catch a trace of his thoughts. But she couldn't. This was a quiet man, she thought, who took his time and did things in slow motion.

The old man returned the picture and said, rolling his eyes, 'Sorry, never seen it before.'

He turned around and walked back into the shadows.

Mei bit her lip. For another minute she watched the old man randomly rearranging his stock. The boy escorted her to the door and said, 'Please walk slowly.'

In one shop after another, the same thing happened. No one would tell Mei anything.

Frustrated, she decided to break for lunch. She headed east towards Forward Gate, where one could find hundreds of restaurants, ranging from the most expensive Original Peking Duck to small home-cooking establishments.

Little shops crammed the narrow *hutongs*. Goods overhung from low roofs like United Nations flags. People from all walks of life had come to the area to shop. Grannies carrying bamboo baskets, usually in pairs, hunted for small household goods like batteries, washing-up liquid and steel cooking knives as long as bricks. They waved the knives in the air, then tested them in shaving motions on their palms.

'Not sharp,' they told the shopkeeper.

'You've got to be kidding. The manufacturer makes swords for Shaoling monks,' replied the young vendor. He pulled out a bamboo stick and swiftly chopped off a slice.

Groups of factory men from the provinces, all wearing grey Mao jackets and smoking cigarettes, wandered about excitedly, chatting loudly in their local tongue. Travellers came here to shop before making their connections at the nearby Beijing Train Station. Food vendors and passing cyclists shouted at the tops of their voices.

'Mongolian lamb kebab, no taste, no charge!'

'How much for the bag?'

'I'd rather die.'

'Eight-layer pancakes! Old Beijing taste!'

Mei found a small restaurant with clean tables and sat down by the window. She ordered a portion of spicy beef noodle soup that came in a bowl the size of a little bucket. She ate her noodles and stared through the lacy curtain at the boy who had been following her. Under a cloud of cigarette smoke, three men chattered loudly at the next table, their faces red from drinking.

Mei left the restaurant, going west in brisk steps, heels clicking. Darting around a corner, she paused, glancing back. She went on again, faster. With a few turns, she was back to the wide pedestrian-only street of Liulichang. She stood in the doorway of the first shop she came to and waited.

'Hey, why are you following me?' she asked, leaning against the wooden column at the entrance.

Mei's words caught the young racehorse by surprise. He stopped in his tracks.

'My uncle asked me to,' said the boy, flashing an embarrassed smile.

'Then let's go see him,' Mei told him.

Sitting on a dark rosewood stool in the back room, Mei counted out eight one-hundred-yuan bills, but she didn't hand them over. 'So you *have* seen it?'

'Not exactly. I saw only pictures of it. Well, I think they were of the same bowl.'

'You are not sure?'

'At my age, nothing is sure,' said the old man. 'It was more than two weeks ago. A young man came here with some pictures of the bowl and asked me how much I'd pay for it.' He rubbed his hands as he spoke. 'Young, I mean the small end of fifty.'

'What did you tell him?'

'He said the bowl was from the Han Dynasty. We are talking over eighteen hundred years old! That's what we call "hand-burning goods". The law says that anything from before 1794 cannot be exported, which means no foreigner will buy it. The Chinese can't afford it. But that's not to say there isn't a way to sell it, you know what I mean? It's a risky business, getting it out of China – could be life or death. So I told him if it was real, which he swore on his mother's grave it was, he could be looking at, say, twenty thousand yuan. He never came back.'

The dealer spoke slowly, pausing every now and then, searching for big educated words.

Mei gave the old man a long inspection. His hair had thinned and dried out like rootless grass. His face had a perpetually apologetic look. He ran a biggish shop filled with things no one was interested in buying. Yet he kept piling in more, in the hope that something would make him rich, and the high-flyers would have to look at him differently. Mei thought about the elaborate way he had haggled for the money she was holding. Here was a hustler acting big, she thought. He spoke of 'ways' and 'hand-burning goods'. From the look of him and his store, he had neither the means nor the nerve for them.

'Frankly, I didn't believe him,' said the old man. 'There aren't any real valuable antiques left anymore. My family has been in Liulichang for three generations. In the '50s, they came and bought up anything of value from the shops. Then the Cultural Revolution took care of whatever was left.'

He stopped rubbing his hands together at the words 'Cultural Revolution', and for a moment his eyes lowered.

'Who are *they*?'

'The government – museums, libraries, universities, you name it,' he said. 'Today there are only two ways you can find anything of real value. Either you are a lucky grave robber or a lucky travelling antiques scout. This guy was neither.'

'How do you know?'

'Grave robbers don't operate alone and they usually have a few things to sell. This guy was on his own and he had only one piece. He wasn't a scout either. He knew nothing about antiques. I tested him; he was a total layman.'

'Do you have a name or a hotel?'

The old man shook his head. 'He only said that he's from Luoyang.'

'Can you tell me what he looked like?'

'Let's see, medium height, strong. Big arms – a manual worker, no doubt, maybe a factory man. Not ugly-looking, except for the scar.'

'Where was this scar?'

'On the left side of his forehead, just above the eye. It looked as if someone had cut him up pretty good.'

The old man held out his hand for the money.

'One more thing,' said Mei. 'Who do you think he sold the bowl to?'

'I wouldn't know.'

Mei didn't move.

'All right, there's a shady character called Big Papa Wu in that mansion down the street. He isn't a good dealer but he seems to be doing very well. There's something fishy about the man, if you ask me.'

10

Big Papa Wu stood in the foyer of his spacious shop, letting his weight drop at the halfway point between his two feet. He stared at Mei with empty eyes. He was not a big man, but he was every inch tough. Clean-shaven and crew-cut, Mei made him out to be in his forties, though it was difficult to say whether early or late. He didn't ask who had sent her or why. He just stood there, looking down at her with an icy stare.

She had told him that she worked for a wealthy collector and wanted to talk to him about one of his recent acquisitions, then showed him the same picture she had shown the other dealers.

Big Papa Wu threw a quick glance at the picture and went dead on her. The friendly anticipation of yet another customer vanished into the dark void behind his eyes.

Mei watched as he walked up to a young man behind a pair of blue Ming vase reproductions. Heads together, they looked at her as they spoke. A few minutes later, the two men went off in different directions. Big Papa Wu disappeared into the back. The young man came straight at Mei. The corners of her mouth curled up. She knew that there wasn't much he could do to make her leave. After all, she was a woman, well dressed and soft-shouldered. But she also knew that there was nothing here for her anymore. So she left.

Across the street was a bazaar that sold small items, things like stone seals and antique jewelleries, in trays. The stalls were organised in the shape of an enclosed rectangle inside which sat dealers on high stools or folding chairs.

Mei took off her coat and untied her hair. She pretended to be interested in buying rubbings, while all the time keeping an eye on the entrance to Big Papa Wu's.

His was a two-storey mansion with a raised entrance flanked by long windows, and a balcony on the first floor. The windows and the balcony railings were constructed of thin strips of wood worked into delicate square patterns resembling Chinese characters.

Twenty minutes later Mei saw Big Papa Wu coming out, dressed in a black leather jacket with its collar turned up. He stopped at the top of the steps and lit a cigarette with slow, measured movements. Puffing, he eyed the street in both directions, then walked down the steps, checked the street again, spat between his feet, and turned right.

Mei seized her chance, joining the stream of shoppers drifting towards South Xinhua Street, eyes firmly on Big Papa Wu.

A red taxi did a U-turn and stopped at the entrance to the pedestrian zone. Its light went off and a Chinese woman and a white man emerged. Big Papa Wu waved the cigarette that was sandwiched between his fingers, signalling the driver to bring the taxi around. When it pulled up, Big Papa Wu threw his cigarette on the ground with a jerk of his wrist and got in. The taxi's light lit up. With a cough of black smoke it drove off towards Peace Gate.

Mei rushed to her car.

Shoppers and shopping bags had taken over the steps leading up to the entrance of the Lufthansa Centre. Everywhere was confusion. Friends looked for friends. Families argued about how to get home. A man zigzagged through the crowd peddling watches from inside his coat. Every now and then, a luxury car pulled up in front of the shopping centre to spill out a pretty girl and her *Dakuan* – her Big Money Man.

Big Papa Wu alighted from the taxi and walked slowly up the steps, looking around. He seemed to be searching for someone or something.

Mei drove into the car park and switched off the engine. At the top of the steps, Big Papa Wu stopped. He lit a cigarette.

From a newspaper hut, a loudspeaker was blasting advertisements for the latest edition of the TV guide. Taxi drivers struggled for passengers. Private cars struggled for parking spaces.

Before long, Big Papa Wu made his move. Crushing the cigarette under his heel, he strode down to greet a large black car that had just pulled up. The car door opened. A tall man in a sleek sports jacket stepped out, followed by a leggy young woman of the same height.

The two men shook hands and chatted. The girl was introduced. People turned their heads to stare at the beautiful couple. The chauffeur pointed to a space near the entrance and said something to the man, probably indicating that he would be waiting there. As the car moved off, Mei noticed that it was an Audi, and that it had a Beijing licence plate.

Big Papa Wu and the beautiful couple entered the shopping centre.

Mei got out of her car to follow them.

11

Loneliness is what follows us to the end, thought Ling Bai, as her body hit the floor. She heard the sound of china breaking, first a loud bang, then a gentle tinkle. Tofu Flower Soup was now all over the floor, white jelly-like chunks wobbling on top of thick brown broth. Two steamed buns rolled down towards the bookshelf. The room suddenly filled with the smell of food.

Ling Bai stretched out her hand, trying to grab the leg of the table in order to pull her body closer to the red telephone, covered by a handkerchief on the small table in the entrance hall. She could already feel the pain subsiding from the left side of her body and knew that in a matter of minutes she would not be able to move at all. Her heart was thumping. She gasped, and gasped again, but could not breathe. She reached out like a drowning woman calling for help.

She lay with her head on the cold floor. She remembered the spring coming through her kitchen window, a square-metre opening in a six-storey matchbox. She thought of the unfinished painting in her studio. It was a traditional subject: a cat playing with a ball in a rock garden. She had stood in front of it, contemplating the composition, while her meat buns were steaming on the stove.

Sunshine had leaked into the living room. The day was now transparent and lightweight. Ling Bai felt her body floating up into the brightness and peace beyond. She closed her eyes and stopped struggling.

Yet the pain, earthly and heavy, began to pull her back down, to remind her of the darkness of death. Ling Bai twitched involuntarily and groaned. She didn't mind dying. But she didn't want to leave before she was forgiven.

12

As she reached the top of the stairs, Mei's mobile phone rang, startling her. Instead of answering it she pushed open the glass door, stepping into a white cosmetic hall. Gorgeous Shiseido and Dior posters faced her. Sales ladies in perfect make-up were murmuring about creams and lipsticks. There was no sign of Big Papa Wu and his friends. Mei looked around in annoyance, wondering how they could have disappeared so quickly and where she should start looking. Her mobile rang again.

This time she answered it, trying to keep her voice to a whisper. 'Who is it?'

It was Gupin, shouting. His accent was heavier than usual.

'Calm down. I can't understand what you're saying.'

'Quickly, Mei! Something has happened to your mother.'

Twenty minutes later, Mei was racing down the busy streets of Chaoyang in her red Mitsubishi. At the entrance to the ring-road, she halted, blocked by a traffic jam as taxis and private cars fought to get onto the freeway. Mei honked, long and loud.

The ring-road opened, like a knife gleaming under the blue sky. Mei passed the Bridge of Three Elements and other places she remembered well on the way to her mother's apartment.

Years ago, when she was a senior at university, she did a bike tour of the east coast. She had answered an advertisement on a campus noticeboard which said: 'Three male political science graduate students seek three female students to join them for a bicycle trip to attend the anniversary of Tangshan earthquake. Must be fun and adventurous.'

Two hundred thousand people had died in that earthquake in 1976. Fun and adventure were not exactly the words that came to mind. But Mei answered the ad anyway. The trip took the six of them beyond Tangshan. After three weeks and eight hundred kilometres, two of their bikes were beyond repair. The girls were exhausted. They flagged down a truck to carry them on the last leg of their journey and arrived at the Bridge of Three Elements in Beijing covered in mosquito bites and minor bruises. She still had a photo of the six of them, smiling triumphantly, on top of the bridge, their bicycles piled somewhere on the pavement like scrap metal.

It used to be the road leading home for Mei. Back then it was the symbol of Beijing's newfound prosperity. There were still green fields to the north of the road. Where is home now? Mei wondered. She and Lu had moved out of her mother's apartment a long time ago. As more high-rises were built, the landscape along the road changed into new and unrecognisable shapes. So had their lives.

Mei hadn't been able to find out what exactly had happened to Mama. The maid, who had called Mei's office, was hysterical. Mei had immediately telephoned for an ambulance to go to her mother's apartment, then dialled Auntie Zhao's number.

Auntie and Uncle Zhao had been their neighbours for almost twenty years.

Few words were exchanged when Auntie Zhao called back to tell Mei that the ambulance had come and that she was going with it to the hospital.

'I'll see you there,' Mei said and hung up.

Mei left the ring-road at West Garden, and was quickly caught up in the slow, narrow streets of Haidian district. There were shops and vending booths on both sides of the road. Bicycles in their hundreds pressed along the middle, sometimes completely filling the gaps between buses and cars. Horse carts moved slowly, despite the peasants cracking their whips and shouting 'Ja Ja.'

After the Summer Palace, the West Mountains appeared. The Grand Canal, lined with white aspen trees, flowed unassumingly at the bottom of the mountain. No more mad constructions and crowded shops. No more city uniformity. The air was fresher and colder.

On that quiet riverbank, deep in the shades of aspen, Mei remembered a little girl, about ten years old, engrossed in a search for white mushrooms that had sprung up after a warm rain.

'Mama, are these the right ones?' She ran up to her mother, some metres ahead, shaking her pigtails with excitement, eyes wide.

'They are just the kind we are looking for,' said her mother, taking in the mushrooms with a deep breath. Daughter and mother bore an astonishing resemblance: the way they curled the corners of their mouths when they spoke and the straightness of their noses – a little too sharp, some said.

Oh, how her mother had smiled at her! How young she was,

and how young they both were! Mei's breath became shorter, her heartbeat faster. She could hardly hold the steering wheel. She felt that her insides were going to burst out of her body. Tears poured down her face. Those happy days blurred before her mind's eye.

No. 309 Hospital was one of the four military hospitals in Beijing. An angry-looking receptionist rolled her eyes crossly when Mei asked her where the emergency room was. 'First floor,' she answered brusquely. Mei made her way up the stairs without waiting for the lift. There were four darkened hallways. Tired relatives lay on benches, squatted or sat on the floor. Some were eating.

Mei followed the sign for the emergency room onto a skywalk bridging two buildings. A thundering noise rolled towards her and she jumped to one side. A trolley was speeding down the ramp, boiling water spilling from the spouts of kettles. Wrapped in a cloud of steam, a worker was running beside the trolley, trying to balance it. Another worker at the back pulled the handlebar as hard as he could to slow it down.

Auntie Zhao was outside the emergency room. Seeing Mei, she staggered over on her cane. Mei reached out to help her, but instead found herself pulled forward to Auntie Zhao's chest. Mei was surprised by the strength of the tiny woman.

'You poor girl!' said Auntie Zhao as she embraced her.

In the arms of this thin-limbed lady whom she had known for twenty years, Mei felt as if she had come to the end of a journey. The ocean behind her had ceased roaring, and like a battered boat at harbour she broke down.

'She's been inside for a while now. The doctors and nurses are all there.' Tears were welling inside Auntie Zhao's eyes also. She turned her head to one side for a moment to conceal them, and asked Mei whether Lu was coming.

Lu! In the rush to get to the hospital, Mei hadn't even thought to call her.

Lu's assistant answered her phone. He told Mei that her sister was in the studio recording her show.

'I will let her know as soon as she comes out,' the assistant's trained impersonal voice assured her.

Mei sat down with Auntie Zhao.

'When I got there, I saw her lying on the living room floor, breakfast spilled everywhere,' said Auntie Zhao. 'There was white foam on her lips. She was twitching. I tried to talk to her. I thought she wanted to say something, but nothing came out. I told her not to worry and that you'd called the ambulance. The maid was crying and saying that she wanted to go home. I told her to shut up and start cleaning up the place. Then the ambulance came.'

'Thank you for helping. Especially for coming to the hospital.'

'Of course. Don't even mention it.'

The emergency room door swung open. Noises, a bed and three nurses came out. One of them was pushing the bed, one holding a drip, and one carrying oxygen. A couple of doctors followed behind.

'Mama!' Mei stopped the moving bed.

But her mother did not respond. There were tubes attached to her nose, arms and mouth. She looked like a broken machine being taped together again.

'She is still unconscious. Are you her daughter?' The younger of the two doctors came up to her.

'What happened to her?' asked Mei without taking her eyes off her mother, who looked dry and lifeless, as if she might fade away any minute.

'She had a stroke. It was bad. Could I talk to you in my office?'

'Where are you taking her?' Mei held on to the bed.

'Room 206 in Building No. 3.'

'I will go with them.' Auntie Zhao hopped over on her cane.

The young doctor's office was a windowless room at the end of the hall. Three men in white coats were watching a small TV fixed to the wall.

'Get out, get out,' the doctor said to them. 'I need to talk to the relatives.'

The other white-coats paid no attention to Mei at all. Slowly they got up, teacups in hand, and left the room, chatting.

The doctor looked to be in his mid-thirties. A pair of dark-framed glasses sat clumsily on his nose.

'We've done everything we could and now it is up to her. She may improve or not,' said the doctor after they sat down.

'When will we know?' asked Mei.

'We should have a better idea in the next few days – it's hard to say when, exactly.'

'What are her chances?'

'Hard to say,' the doctor said again. 'Wait and see, okay?'

Then the doctor cleared his throat, preparing to deliver a speech he had made many times before. 'Sorry to be bringing up the cost issue at this time. But you do understand, don't you? If your mother's condition worsens, she will need intensive care and treatment. Will you be able to pay the costs yourselves? If you are able to pay privately, we can use imported drugs straight away.'

The doctor looked up, but not exactly at Mei. His glance was focused on something beyond, somewhere ambiguous.

'What about her medical insurance?' Mama had been an employee of the government all her life, a Party member. She must have benefits. She certainly should have.

'I'm afraid your mother's ranking is not high enough,' said the doctor, now looking at Mei.

Mei felt the scrutiny of those shallow eyes. They seemed to be implying that her mother was some sort of failure, her life unimportant.

'When do we need to decide?' Mei asked, trying to hold back her rage. She wanted the best treatment and care for her mother. But she did not have that kind of money. Medical bills, depending on how long her mother would need to be hospitalised, could really add up. She needed to speak to Lu.

'Any time, really. When you are ready, just come to see me and sign the paper.'

On her way back to her mother, Mei tried Lu again. Her assistant responded with a bit more warmth this time. 'She is coming out of the studio right now.'

Mei updated her sister on what had happened. She could hear Lu crying at the other end. 'Of course, I will pay whatever the cost. Mama will have the best treatment. I'll sign anything. I'm coming as soon as I can.'

13

When Mei reached room 206 in Building No. 3, her mother was asleep. A battered yellowish aluminium mug stood on her nightstand. An aluminium spoon lay inside. A large red Thermos bottle had been left at the foot of the nightstand. It had a pink plum blossom painted on it and Critical I written in black ink.

The patient in the next bed, an elderly woman, was about to have dinner. She had a weathered face from a lifetime working in the fields. Her hair was short and yet still pinned back. It can't have been easy to do up all those pins, Mei thought. A young girl who looked like her granddaughter had come with a bag full of food. She took out an apple and tossed it over. Like an outfielder, the old woman caught the flying apple in mid-air. Mei wondered what kind of life-threatening illness had brought *her* here. Judging from their provincial accents, Mei guessed that they were relatives of some military people stationed in Beijing. They had probably used their connections to get the old woman put in here; rooms for critically ill patients were better equipped than the wards, and only shared by two people.

Mei walked Auntie Zhao to the door and thanked her again. She then went back to her mother's side and sat down on a plastic stool.

More people had come to see the old woman. Sweet buns, sausages, pancakes started to fly across. Perhaps because of their loud talk and laughter, or maybe because the anaesthetic had worn off, Ling Bai groaned and woke up.

'Mama,' Mei cried, seizing her mother's bony hand and raising her voice to make sure her mother could hear her. 'I am here.'

Ling Bai opened her eyes slowly, starting to focus. 'Lu,' she muttered weakly but unmistakably. Her lips were blistered and dry – like the wound of a dead animal, Mei thought.

'No, Mama, it's Mei.'

Mei held her mother's hand and felt the softness of her skin, the warmth of a human being, alive. Mei wanted to pull her close, to hug her, to hold her tightly in her arms.

Presently a nurse came in to check on the drip and the patient's pulse. She fixed the oxygen tubes. 'Don't let her move too much,' she told Mei without explaining why.

'You –' she turned to look severely at the crowd around the neighbouring bed, 'be quiet. This patient needs rest.'

Then, without another word to Mei, she left the room.

Ling Bai slipped in and out of consciousness as Mei stroked the hand she was holding.

'Mei,' she heard her mother call.

'Yes, Mama. I am here.'

Ling Bai opened her eyes. This time they were more focused. She looked at Mei.

'Where is Lu?' she asked.

'She is on her way, Mama. Would you like some water?' Mei wiped sweat from her mother's forehead.

Ling Bai seemed to nod and then closed her eyes again.

Mei took half a spoonful of cooled boiled water from the aluminium mug and brought it to her mother's dry lips. It took Ling Bai a long time to take in a little bit of water.

'Enough?' Mei asked when she saw her mother's mouth twitching.

She thought Ling Bai said, 'Yes,' but could not be sure. She moved her ear closer to those dried-out lips, but speaking appeared to have exhausted her mother.

Mei put the hospital mug and spoon back on the nightstand and marched over to the increasingly raucous crowd around the old woman's bed.

'Please be quiet! My mother has just had a stroke. She needs rest. Don't you even care?' She had to raise her voice against the noise they were making.

But Mei knew that they didn't care. She couldn't stand people who had no respect for others. Her mother had always said that she was too hard and had too many edges. 'Either you don't talk at all or talk too harshly, offending people either way. No wonder you have no people luck.'

No, no luck at all, thought Mei. Not in life or in love.

Suddenly the door opened and Lu came in. She looked exquisite with her beige skirt suit, long arched eyebrows and flawless make-up. Her hair had been dyed honey brown, and there was a hint of golden highlights around her face. Following closely behind was her personal assistant, the one with whom Mei had spoken earlier. He wore a black suit, had neatly trimmed razor-sharp hair, and was young and handsome.

'Mama, it's Lu.' She went straight to the small stool by the side of the bed and took her mother's hand, pressing it to her rosy cheeks. 'Everything's going to be fine.'

'It's my turn now,' sighed Ling Bai. A single tear appeared at the corner of her eye. She did not want to die, after all.

'No, Mama. Don't worry. I am going to take care of you.' Lu instructed her assistant to find the chief doctor and head nurse. The young man went out. Mei gave her sister another update, mentioning the noisy crowd around the other bed. Ten minutes later, the chief doctor came in person to invite Lu to his office.

After her meeting, Lu pulled Mei to the window and said, 'The doctors think Mama's chance of recovering is small. You know Mama, she's had plenty of health problems. Now the doctor is saying that her liver and kidneys are deteriorating. They don't understand why. It's as if there's a general shutdown.' She paused for a second. 'The chief doctor suggests that we contact all the relatives and Mama's friends, which I will ask my assistant to do. We need to be prepared.'

Mei did not know what to say. She wondered whether you could ever be prepared for the death of your mother.

The head nurse came in shortly, and advised them to hire a worker-help. 'My niece has been doing this for quite a few years,' she said. 'She knows about things such as where to go for help and what to do to ease pain. And she can come and get me at any time.'

It was agreed that they would hire the head nurse's niece. Her duties would include fetching food for Mei and Lu, bringing hot water from the boiler room and massaging Ling Bai's arms and legs, and she would stay for overnight shifts.

The old woman in the next bed checked out around six o'clock that evening. Whether she was due to leave anyway, or whether Lu had used her influence, Mei didn't know.

After dinner time, Ling Bai dozed off again and Lu went home. Her husband was waiting. Mei decided to stay. It might be irrational, but she feared that if she was not around, her mother would slip away into the night, like her father, and be lost forever.

Besides, no one was waiting for her elsewhere.

14

For most of the next day, Ling Bai remained the same, drifting in and out of consciousness. She lay in bed like an empty, abandoned house. Sometimes she opened her eyes. She saw nothing in particular. There was a ceiling fan hanging idly. A fly hopped from the nightstand to the wall, up to the ceiling, to the window, and then back again. It soon grew bored with the routine and attached itself to the ceiling like a permanent stain.

Mei fed her mother water with a spoon. The worker-help had bought new spoons from the hospital shop, along with a white porcelain teacup, two face towels and a cream-coloured washing basin decorated with red and yellow peonies, the national flower. Mei used to have a similar washing basin in her dorm room at university. Every morning and evening she would take it to the washroom to wash her face and sometimes her long silky hair. Though she could not recall its exact colour or the flower pattern on it, she remembered how shiny it had been when her mother brought it home. It had the smell of something brand-new, as fresh as her own young life.

Next to the bed, the worker-help poured hot water from a Thermos into the new washing basin, raising clouds of steam. When the water had cooled, she soaked the towel in it. Then she squeezed the water out, folded the towel a few times, and handed it to Mei. Mei laid the towel on her mother's forehead and leaned over her.

'Are you in pain?' she asked.

'Leg,' Ling Bai answered in a parched voice.

At the bottom of the bed, Mei lifted the quilt. There was a smell of old sweat. Ling Bai's feet were swollen, her toenails thick and black. She had lost all feeling in the left side of her body. Mei gently massaged the calf, knee and thigh of her mother's right leg.

'Better?' she asked.

Ling Bai nodded and sighed silently.

At eleven o'clock, the nurse did her rounds again. She followed the same procedure each time. First, she counted the number of drops by her wristwatch and made an adjustment to the drip. Then she checked the tubes and the patient's temperature. Finally, she shone a torch into her patient's eyes and shouted 'Ling Bai!' She appeared satisfied when Ling Bai responded. 'Has she urinated?' the nurse asked.

After the nurse had left, Ling Bai slept. The worker-help suggested that Mei have lunch, but Mei said she was not hungry.

'Big Sister . . .' The worker-help was clearly older than Mei, but she insisted on calling her Big Sister to show respect. 'Big Sister, I've been around hospitals for twelve years. One thing I do know is that you eat when you can. You don't know which way the wind might blow and when you might eat again.'

She was a likeable woman, with cropped hair, a faded

dark-blue Mao jacket and a square face. Mei smiled, and gave her some money.

'I won't go to the hospital canteen, their food's not good. I go to the vendor outside the front gate,' said the worker-help. She tucked the money carefully in her pocket and left. A while later she came back with three palm-sized meat buns and a bottle of mineral water. Mei ate everything.

Shortly after lunch, Mei went for a walk around the hospital premises. Convalescing patients moved slowly in the warm sunshine like toy figures with broken springs, accompanied by family and friends. A heavily bandaged man limped along, his steps hesitant, stopping often. Two middle-aged peasant women helped a heavy man in a military winter coat to recover the use of his legs; he was spitting in frustration. Everything seemed to be moving at a different pace, everything had its own rhythm. Minutes and hours stretched seemingly forever.

Depressed, Mei turned and headed towards the main entry, passing the emergency entrance. Drivers kept pulling up, pleading special needs, as two uniformed guards shouted and cursed, trying to keep the driveway clear for ambulances.

Once outside, Mei turned left, fending off the hustling of illegal taxi drivers. A hundred yards down the road was a small restaurant, the only one within miles. It had oily plastic table covers and a mean-looking waitress. Mei went around to the back and saw her little red Mitsubishi still parked there. Judging by the number of cars, the restaurant was doing a brisk business from the sick and dying.

The worker-help had suggested that Mei park her car here overnight, which turned out to be more expensive than parking at the Beijing Theatre. But the alternative was to leave it by the roadside, which meant for sure that someone would throw a brick at it in the night. There's capitalism for you, Mei thought – supply and demand, anything justified. She walked into the restaurant and paid for another night's parking.

When she got back to room 206, two men were waiting by the door. Mei recognised Uncle Chen at once; he was wearing a short beige sports jacket, which had shrunk to reveal a worn belt. Mei did not know the other man. He was tall, Mei guessed six foot; he wore a smooth grey suit and a pair of rimless glasses. He was clean-shaven, sober, and looked like a bookish man who'd never put a foot wrong in his life.

'Lu called me. I am so sorry,' Uncle Chen said.

'Sorry to hear about your mother.' The bookish man shook her hand. 'We went in to see her, but she was sleeping. We didn't want to disturb her rest.' He spoke in a warm voice. Mei put him at about her mother's age. He continued to hold her hand, firm and sincere. She thought he was probably a deputy Party secretary at her mother's work unit, or maybe a director for Elderly Comrade Affairs – they were the usual types sent on hospital rounds.

'We've spoken to the doctor,' he said. 'Don't worry. The Party has not forgotten. We'll take care of things.'

Bookish finally released his clasp. It was not hard to see that he had been handsome in his youth. 'Mr Song Kaishan is an old comrade who used to work with your mother and me,' Uncle Chen said.

Mr Song interrupted. 'Old Chen, we must leave now.' To Mei he said, 'Please give your mother my best wishes.' He shook Mei's hand again, this time briefly.

'Give me a call if you need anything,' Uncle Chen murmured. Mei felt he wanted to say more. He hesitated, turned, and quietly followed Mr Song's elegant steps. Mei watched them fade into the dark corridor. A strange sensation came over her. She felt as if cold air had risen from nowhere and, like a ghost, had tapped her with its invisible hand.

Lu came in the afternoon, bringing Little Auntie, who had flown in from Shanghai. Little Auntie carried a small leather overnight bag with her. Her eyes were red.

Mei brought a plastic stool for Little Auntie to sit on and took the bag from her.

'Sister, I've come.' Little Auntie broke into Shanghai dialect and took her sister's hand, which lay motionless on the bed.

'Not this one. All the drips are in this arm.' Mei directed Little Auntie to Ling Bai's right hand, the one that still had feeling. She then checked the needles on the left arm to make sure they were still taped and working. The arm looked bruised and swollen. Little Auntie gently stroked her sister's hand.

'Don't give up, Sister. You will get better, and when you do, we will go back to Shanghai. We will go to the New World for Big Won Ton Soup. We will go back to home village to visit Ma's grave.' As she spoke, her silent tears began to choke her.

Ling Bai slowly opened her eyes.

'Little Third,' she murmured. He mouth moved again, but no more sound came.

'Sister, I've come to look after you as you've done for me for so long. You will get better,' Little Auntie said determinedly. Gently she released her sister's hand.

Little Auntie took her black bag and stood up. All three women moved to the patient's locker near the door.

'Thank you for coming,' said Mei. 'Is this okay with your work unit?'

'It's not busy in the lab at the moment. A week should be no problem.' Little Auntie was a lab engineer at the Shanghai Institute for Biological Research.

At that moment, Lu's assistant came in and told her that he had booked a room for Little Auntie at the hospital hotel for one week. 'It's basic but decent,' he said in a matter-of-fact way, handing Lu a tagged key. 'This is the key and the luggage is already in the room.'

After Lu had talked to her mother – first about Lining, who was about to go on his annual trip to North America, and then about her new TV show – she went with her assistant to find the doctor. Mei introduced the worker-help and showed Little Auntie how to feed Mama water. She also told Little Auntie that her mother had been complaining about pain in her leg and showed her how to give a massage.

Lu returned shortly and said that the doctor did not have much more to report. 'All they can do is continue to monitor Mama,' she said.

'Go have some rest. You both have to work tomorrow,' said Little Auntie, sitting down on the plastic stool. 'I'm here now.'

'If anything happens, call. Use the mobile phone I gave you,' Lu told her.

Little Auntie nodded. 'Don't worry.'

'It's good that Little Auntie could come so quickly,' Mei said to her sister as they walked out of the building.

Lu agreed. 'I told Little Auntie that money was no issue for me. I can pay all her expenses, the flight, the hotel and the meals. The problem for me is time. If she hadn't come today either you or I would have had to stay. You may be able to, being your own boss, but I have to keep up with schedules. There are cases to review and people to interview.'

Mei walked Lu to her car. Her assistant was already waiting.

'Did Mama ever work with Uncle Chen?' Mei asked.

'No. Why?'

'Uncle Chen seemed to suggest that they used to be colleagues.'

'Impossible,' said Lu firmly. 'They would have mentioned it if they had.'

Mei nodded. Lu was right. Uncle Chen must have made a mistake. But all the way home she was troubled. The image of the elegant stranger kept coming back to her, casting a dark shadow over her thoughts.

15

Mei slept badly. Her mother's face, shrivelled in pain, appeared in her dreams. The next morning, when she woke from her nightmare, her body ached and her head was pounding. She was exhausted.

As soon as she got up she called Little Auntie at the hospital. They spoke for only a minute. Her mother was awake. Little Auntie assured Mei that nothing had changed since the previous afternoon.

Mei made a cup of coffee and drank it while watching the morning news. The coffee did little for her headache. At nine-thirty she went to work; she was ready for work, and she needed to work. She had to stay busy to keep her mind off her mother. Otherwise, she felt, the weight of her anxiety and fear would simply crush her.

Mei parked her car under the oak tree. Across the yard, Gupin's Flying Pigeon was chained to the young aspen in its usual position. The sun was shining, as it had been for the past two days.

Mei sat in her car for a while with the engine off. She thought she heard birds singing, but when she listened again she heard only the noise of the city, of cars and people. Life was going on as usual; it made Mei want to cry. Would Mama see sunshine and days like this again?

The caretaker had his feet up on the table in the boiler room, listening to the radio.

'Your hot water is already taken up,' he told Mei when she passed. She nodded.

Gupin was sitting at his computer, typing. Seeing Mei, he stood up.

'What happened? Is your mother all right?' he asked.

Mei shook her head. 'She had a stroke. My aunt is with her now in the hospital.'

'I've been really worried. When you didn't come in yesterday, I thought it must be bad.' Gupin paused, his eyes warming. 'But don't worry. She'll get better, just you wait and see. You look tired. Let me get you some tea.'

Mei nodded. She tried to smile, but her mood failed her.

She walked into her office. From the window she could see the top of the oak tree and, fifty metres away, another four-storey building identical to hers. The two buildings had been built by the People's Liberation Army in the early 1970s, when intellectuals and their teenage children were sent to labour camps and People's Collective Communes. They were functional, nothing more. Over the years, they had been defaced by graffiti and pollution.

Mei opened the window. A gentle breeze drifted in like a long-forgotten memory.

Gupin brought in tea, mail and messages.

'My ma had a tumour once,' he told her. 'It was years ago. She complained about her bad headaches. We took her to see the doctor in the county town, Dr Yao, who said she had a tumour in her brain. We all thought she wouldn't make it, the doctor too. But Ma lived. She lost the use of her legs and one of her arms is not so good. But she lived. The doctor said it was because she'd been working all her life. Your mother is like my ma. She's got a strong mind and a good body. She'll be all right.'

Mei knew that Gupin was trying to cheer her up. But cheerfulness seemed to come easily to him. The smallest things made him happy – a blue sky, bicycle bells in the morning, the change of seasons, even the height of skyscrapers.

'Unfortunately, my mother isn't strong in her mind,' Mei said, thinking of the tears Mama had shed over the years. 'She's shouldered a lot of burdens. And she's not an optimist.' I could be talking about myself, she thought.

'You don't want optimism. That's no use. You have to listen to fate. That was what Ma did. It was her fate to live and to have a devoted son like my brother. She thinks it was fate, too, that my brother should marry Lotus, my sister-in-law. Lotus hates Ma. She can't wait for Ma to die so she can become the lady of the house herself. But I'm not going to let her. She says I'm disobedient and that I don't care for Ma. But I send money home. Otherwise how could we afford the herbalists for Ma or to rebuild our family house?'

'You are helping, Gupin. Even though you're not there to look after her. I am sure your mother thinks the same,' Mei said gently.

Her words floated soothingly into her own thoughts. I am a dutiful daughter, she told herself, and Mama knows it.

But her confidence quickly evaporated, leaving her with only doubts and a feeling of reproach. Yes, she had loved her mother and cared for her. She had also disobeyed her. She had caused pain with her failure and single-mindedness. She had brought Mama misery and worry. They had fought. They had hurt each other with their words and deeds.

Mei felt her head starting to throb again. 'Let's get to work,' she said abruptly.

There was no consolation that Gupin or anyone could offer. No one could calm her fears. Time was slipping away. The time that she needed to make Mama love her again was escaping from her fingers like sand.

Mei shut herself inside her office for most of the day. She worked through old files and dealt with bits and pieces from the past two days. She ran through her notes and her memory of her visit to Liulichang and the Lufthansa Centre. Mei wished she had taken a closer look at the man Big Papa Wu met. She remembered him being tall, stylishly dressed and white-skinned, about the same age as Big Papa Wu. Clearly he was rich, going by the car, the chauffeur and the model girlfriend. Mei tried to imagine their conversation over tea in one of the cafés in the basement. They probably talked about the Han ceremonial bowl, and about Mei asking questions.

Mei decided she must find the seller of the ceremonial bowl, and soon.

She opened the door and called out, 'Gupin, could you come in, please?'

When her secretary entered she gestured for him to sit down on the sofa.

'What do you know about the train coming from Luoyang to Beijing?'

'I know a lot about it – that's the train I took to come to the city. There is only one train a day. It gets in to Beijing West Station at five-thirty in the morning. I remember it like it was yesterday. I came in February, after Chinese New Year. When the train arrived, it was still dark out, and I had to wait in the station for daybreak. Once it was light and the buses started running I followed the directions I was given. I took three buses to see a young man from a neighbouring village who had come to Beijing a year earlier. He said I could stay with him and work on the same construction site. I was so excited to see Beijing for the first time – the high buildings, the buses, the wide streets and street-sweeping trucks. I'd never seen street-sweeping trucks before.'

'If you hadn't known this man from your neighbouring village, where would you have stayed?'

'I'd probably have gone to one of the cheap hotels around the station. Many travellers do. Sometimes you can even rent a room from a local resident for as little as fifteen yuan a night. Of course, it's illegal for residents to rent out rooms, since it's their work units, not they, who own the apartments. But you know how it is – people need money.'

'I'm looking for someone from Luoyang. He came to Beijing a couple of weeks ago to sell a valuable antique. All I have of him is a description. He might have stayed in the station area, as you suggest. But I'm sure he's not there anymore. He's rich now, having sold his antique.'

'But someone in the station area may remember him,' Gupin reasoned. 'Perhaps a waitress or the hotel people. They might know where he's gone.'

Mei thought for a while.

'You could also check with the Valuable Item Deposit department at the train station,' Gupin added. 'He would have needed to store his antique somewhere safe. Those cheap hotels are all privately operated, most of them shady – only fools would leave valuables there.'

'I think you're right,' Mei said. 'I'll start at the station.'

'Would you like me to come with you?' asked Gupin. 'The station area is not safe at night. It's full of travellers and local thugs.'

'That's very kind of you, but I think I should do this by myself. Sometimes people will tell a woman more if she is alone.'

Gupin was disappointed. His head dropped. The air of excitement that had surrounded him disappeared.

'Maybe next time.' Mei smiled. 'I'll see you tomorrow.'

16

Outside, twilight had begun to fall. It was the time when the city unwound its springs. Children had gone home following an afternoon of playing cards or football on street kerbs. Dinner tables were being laid. From half-opened kitchen windows, one could smell the sweet summons of grandmothers' cooking.

It was the best time to call someone.

'Oh, Mei!' exclaimed Auntie Chen when she picked up the phone. 'My poor child,' she sighed. 'I hope you're not too worried. Your Uncle Chen has just come back from the hospital. Your mother seems to be doing all right. Keep your heart open wide, okay?'

Uncle Chen came on the line. He gave Mei an update on her mother's condition.

'Thank you for going to see her,' she said. 'I hope to go there tomorrow.'

'Don't worry. How was your meeting with Pu Yan?' Uncle Chen lowered his voice. 'Have you found out anything?'

'That's exactly why I'm calling,' Mei said. 'I went to

Liulichang Antique Market, as Pu Yan had heard that the bowl had been sold to a dealer there. I spoke to someone who remembered the man trying to sell it. He was from Luoyang, as you suspected. But all I could get was a description.

'The dealer is called Big Papa Wu, and he is particularly nasty. I trailed him to the Lufthansa Centre, where he met someone. Unfortunately I couldn't follow them. But I copied down the licence plate of the car and I've asked a friend at the Motor Vehicle Bureau to run it through their system. I suspect our man from Luoyang is still in Beijing. Pu Yan said the ceremonial bowl might have fetched forty thousand yuan. That's a lot of money. Why leave Beijing without sampling the high life?'

'But how are you going to find him? There are ten million people in Beijing.' Uncle Chen sounded worried.

'I'll go back to the beginning – Beijing West Train Station. Can you find me a *Guanxi* into the station? The higher his position, the better.'

'When do you want to go?'

'Tonight. We'd better hurry. I think we have disturbed the grass. The snakes are scared.'

'Let me make a few phone calls,' said Uncle Chen. 'Where are you?'

'In my office.'

'I'll call you back.'

Half an hour later the call came. Mei wrote down the information on a piece of paper, which she then folded and tucked into her wallet. She put her wallet, a bottle of pepper spray and a small torch in a black nylon handbag. She made sure that her mobile phone was sufficiently charged. Then she tossed the handbag over her shoulder and walked out.

*

The wind had died. The clouds thickened, huddled together like a cosy blanket. Lights came on, illuminating Beijing West Train Station, a new building in the shape of an ancient city gate with four pagoda towers. In front of it, people sat on their luggage and waited for buses. Food vendors walked through the crowd shouting, 'Hungry? Eat hot meat buns!'

Inside the station, fresh faces and excited eyes marvelled at the gleaming décor. There was a constant stream of announcements from loudspeakers, telling of departures, delays, lost children and adults. Migrant workers were running everywhere, sacks over their shoulders. Families huddled together in white waiting rooms, sharing paper-box dinners of stir-fry on rice. Others slept, stretched out like corpses on the long benches.

Mei stopped outside the stationmaster's office. A sign on the door read: No Drifters.

She pushed the door open. Inside she counted eight people sitting on a long bench by the wall. Mei walked up to the young woman behind the desk and asked to see the stationmaster.

'Do you want to make a complaint?' The woman pushed a glossy magazine to one side and opened her thick eyelids wide. 'Fill out a form and wait over there.'

'No, it's a private matter,' said Mei.

She looked at Mei, rolling her eyes. 'What kind of private matter?' Her voice was now less curt.

Mei leaned over the desk. 'Please tell him that I am a friend of Mr Rong Felin of the Railway Bureau.'

The woman stood up and disappeared through the door behind her desk. Soon Mei heard a chair moving. The door reopened, and a stout man in grey and red railway uniform stepped forward to greet her. His eager smiles arrived before his hand. 'Please come in,' he said. They shook hands.

'I'm Wang Mei,' she said.

'My name is Li Gou. I am the deputy stationmaster. The stationmaster has gone home. How can I help?' He had a mouthful of brown teeth.

'Xiao Yang,' he said to the woman from the desk, 'tea.'

Xiao Yang nodded and left.

'Please, do sit down. What a terrible day, suddenly cold again.' Mr Li pulled up a chair to sit near Mei. 'How is Comrade Rong these days? I used to work for him. Well, not directly. It was when he was the stationmaster at Beijing Station and I was one of his passenger managers. Then Comrade Rong was promoted to the Railway Bureau. I don't know whether he would remember me. Before I came here I ran the Beijing–Guangdong line.'

Mei smiled and said nothing.

'Well, well.' He showed his teeth to Mei again, smoothing down his uniform. 'Let's talk about what it is you need.'

'I am looking for a man who came to Beijing from Luoyang two weeks ago. He might have stored something of value in your Valuable Item Deposit. I'd like to see the records.'

'Of course,' said Mr Li. He got up and went behind his desk to consult his records.

Tea was brought in. Xiao Yang poured a cup for Mr Li and another for Mei, then left.

Mr Li opened a large notebook and ran his finger across and down the pages. Finding the page he wanted, he said, 'The duty supervisor at luggage deposit tonight is . . . eh, Tang Yi. I'll ask Xiao Yang to take you there.'

He picked up his teacup and came back to sit by Mei.

'I am afraid that the person who did the check-in might not be there tonight. There are usually two shifts, one in the morning and one in the evening. I am not sure how exactly they run the shifts over there. Sometimes they switch people around. Tang Yi can give you the details.'

'Could I go there now?' asked Mei, leaving her tea untouched.

'Of course, as you wish,' said Mr Li, standing up.

'I will tell Comrade Rong that you have been helpful,' Mei said.

'Thank you. If I can be of any further assistance, just let me know.' The brown teeth opened in a grin.

Mei followed Xiao Yang to the luggage deposit. A small crowd had formed in front of the counter; it was hard to judge where the end of the queue was or whether there had even been one. Two identical-looking women steered the mob with as little talking or eye contact as possible. Their uniforms were carelessly buttoned. They snapped at their customers like anxious cats. They were at the end of their shifts.

'Didn't I tell you to go to the side? I don't need your identity card *now*. First fill out the form!' yelled the older of the twins.

Xiao Yang went up to her and asked for their supervisor, and was told that he was in the back.

Mr Tang jumped up when Xiao Yang and Mei entered. He tried to extinguish his cigarette with one hand and put on his cap with the other.

'Xiao Yang, what wind has blown you over my way?' His smile was wide.

'Miss Wang is from the Railway Bureau,' Xiao Yang said frostily. 'She needs to see your records. Stationmaster Li asks you to assist her as best you can, and wants to know how it works out.'

She then said a friendly goodbye to Mei.

Mr Tang's eyes rolled as they followed Xiao Yang out of the door. He tossed his railway cap back onto the desk and lit another cigarette. He wasn't keen to help Mei or anyone. He was obviously cross that his boss had burdened him with such a tiresome task. His face was pale and he looked as if he needed a drink.

He leaned back on the edge of the desk, blowing smoke through his yellow fingers. 'What are you looking for?'

'I'd like to see the records for your Valuable Item Deposit going back two weeks,' said Mei. 'And then I'd like to speak with your workers.'

Mr Tang sucked on his cigarette. He walked over to a cabinet and started pulling out files.

'I keep only the last four weeks in this office,' he murmured, the cigarette dangling at the corner of his mouth. Thin smoke hung around him like a jealous lover. 'The rest gets shipped out to records. You'd think these days few people have real valuables that they'd want to pay extra to leave with us. You'd be surprised. All kinds of junk gets stashed in here.'

Mr Tang dumped a pile of paper onto the desk in front of Mei. He then went back to his leaning, a new cigarette in his mouth.

Mei started to go through the records. People left all types of things in the Valuable Item Deposit – an ash box, a sealed envelope, a small bundle wrapped in rough cloth, a live bird in a cage. They came from all over the country to leave a piece of their lives here: the paddy fields of the south, the icicle-covered forests of the north-east, the grassland and horses and mountains of the west. Some were from Luoyang, where the Silk Road began. Mei took those records out.

One of the halogen lights flickered. Mr Tang picked up a broom from the corner and hit the shaft to no effect.

'Which department of the Bureau did you say you were from?' he asked.

'I didn't,' said Mei.

Mr Tang fell silent, and stayed so for the next twenty minutes. Finally, Mei looked up and said, 'Could you please ask one of your lady comrades to come and see me?'

Mr Tang squeezed a little space in the ashtray and stubbed out his cigarette. He put on his cap and, with a loud bang of the door, went out.

Mei waited. After a long while, Mr Tang returned with the younger of the twins. She was in her mid-twenties, not pretty but with lively eyes. Her cheeks were red after hours behind the counter and dry from the stale air of the station. She walked in briskly.

'How are you, Comrade Wang?' Her voice was sharp. She held out her hand. 'Old Tang told me that you are from the Bureau. I look after the Valuable Item Deposit. May I sit down?' She pulled a chair over and waited.

Mei turned to Mr Tang. 'Could you excuse us?'

He looked away. With thumb and index finger he picked tobacco from his teeth.

'Please!' Mei ordered.

After a last puff on another cigarette, Mr Tang threw the butt on the floor and ground it under his foot. He then took his hat and left the room.

'Do you remember this man, Zhang Hong?' Mei handed the other woman a sheet of paper. 'It says here that he deposited a large wooden box on the first of April and collected it five days later. The box would have been at least this big.' Mei drew a rectangle with her hands. 'I believe he was of a strong build, medium height and had a scar above his left eye. He had a Henan accent.'

The young woman nodded and held Mei's gaze. As she listened, she assumed the expression of someone searching through a long, winding tunnel of memory.

'He had something very valuable in that box. He may have been nervous or overexcited, acting out of the ordinary,' said Mei. 'I think he would have come here around six in the evening to pick up the box. You run two trains to Hong Kong and Shenzhen every evening at about eight o'clock, don't you?' According to Mei's calculation, that would have given him just enough time to complete the transaction for the ceremonial bowl to go on the next train to the Hong Kong region.

The woman pouted, tilting her head to the side, and closing her eyes. Mei imagined her silently remembering each day, combing through faces that had no meaning until now.

Mei went on, hoping something she had said or was about to say might stir the woman's memory. 'He had come to Beijing for the first time. He had a big plan. He had come to get rich. I'd guess he had a new wardrobe for the occasion – new shoes, new clothes, new haircut, new bags, the whole works.'

The woman opened her eyes. They were unfocused. They closed and opened again. Then she spoke.

'I think I remember now. He had a big scar, like it was done by a machine.' She squinted. 'Yes, he had on a new suit, but it looked cheap. He carried a leather toiletry bag, the way people from the provinces do.'

She gave Mei a knowing smile. 'I've worked on the railways for many years. It's always the same.' Her thoughts had reached the end of the tunnel; lights were coming on. Her memory began to speed up.

'They all try to look smart when they come to a big city like Beijing, with new hairdos and new clothes that are fashionable in their own cities. But they all end up looking like animals from the zoo. I can smell the dirt in them from a *li* away. So at first I didn't pay attention to what's his name, Zhang Hong.'

'But you did notice him.'

'Eventually I did. Why? Yes, I remember it now. It was quite busy that evening. I told him that everybody was in a hurry and that he would have to wait in the back. He fidgeted and complained, sometimes about the service, sometimes about something else. I hate such people. Who are they to tell us that we don't offer good service?

'I remember it now, as clearly as if it had happened yesterday. When I finally got the box out for him, he shouted at me with a heavy accent – possibly Henan, I don't know – "Careful, careful, terribly valuable."

'They all think that they've got this gold or that treasure, when in fact it's not worth a dime. We get a lot of people like that coming through here. Do you know that our West Station is the largest in Asia? Sometimes there are three of us; sometimes, like today, just two. People don't know what's going on, they don't understand or are too stupid, they are late and want their things. They curse and try to give us orders. We serve the people, but we are not servants.'

Her eyes glowed as she became more and more animated.

'As I was saying, I got pretty angry. I put the box on the counter and asked him to sign the release. He went crazy, screaming, "Heavens, don't slam it!" I didn't even put it down with a heavy hand. I'd had it up to here.' She lifted her right arm and hit her chin with the back of her hand.

'So I told him to read the notice on the wall: "Deposit at your own risk. The West Station is not responsible for any damages".'

'What happened then?'

'Well, nothing. The person who was with him told him they had to go. So they took the box and left.'

Mei looked up. 'He had a friend with him? Was he someone quite muscular with a crew cut?'

'No.' She shook her head. 'It was a young girl.'

'A young girl?' Mei had not expected this. 'What kind of girl? How old was she?'

'Maybe eighteen. You know – the kind with permed hair: a slut.'

'Was she a Beijinger?'

'If she had an accent, I didn't notice it.'

Mei breathed deeply. She'd heard all she wanted to hear. 'Thank you. You've been very helpful,' she said. 'Keep what we've talked about to yourself, understand?'

'No sweat. It's our duty to help comrades from the Bureau.' The girl got up and shook hands. Mei noticed that they were trembling with excitement.

After she left, Mr Tang came back in. A cigarette was attached to his fingers like an additional limb. He studied Mei thoughtfully.

She said, 'Thank you, Mr Tang. I won't trouble you any longer.' As she touched his bony yellow hand, Mei felt a chill in her spine.

17

Though the government required everyone who planned to stay in Beijing for more than three days to register with the police, plenty of people didn't. Someone like Zhang Hong certainly wouldn't have. Even using his identity card number, it was unlikely that Mei would be able to trace him through police records.

But the news that he was with a Beijing girl was promising. The fact that she knew Zhang Hong before he sold the antique suggested that she might be someone who worked in the area, perhaps a waitress or a chambermaid. He had probably boasted about the money he was going to get, and made her promises.

Mei watched her back as she walked into the unlit streets a couple of blocks away from the station. Here the narrow alleyways and courtyard houses of old Beijing had been replaced by reinforced concrete erected in the 1950s and 1960s when the government steamrolled the New Five Year Plans. Now these buildings stood laced with time's decay. Soon they would be knocked down to make way for a new vision.

The night had become dangerous and cold. There were faint murmurs rustling behind old piles of furniture. Figures moved soundlessly in the shadows. A yellow light bulb hung over the entrance to a small guesthouse, illuminating a sign saying 'No Vacancies'.

The guesthouse was a two-storey building, with grey plastered walls. It was an extension of some kind, probably built in a hurry from poor materials. Mei could not tell from what it had extended or what other purpose it might have served before it was turned into a guesthouse. Somewhere to the right, on the first floor, a pale glow wavered behind a window.

An old woman was sitting at the reception desk knitting the sleeve of a very small jumper. Every now and then, she crossed the knitting needles and laid the jumper on her lap. She measured the length of the sleeve using the distance between her thumb and middle finger.

'For your *waisun* – your daughter's son?' Mei asked. The sight of the tiny woolly knit and the woman's face made her think of her mother.

'No, for my *sunzi* – my son's son!' The woman spoke in a soft southern accent, a sound like clear water running through green streams. Pride filled her wrinkles.

'How old is he?'

'Oh, no. He is not born yet.' She stroked the sweater as if it were a child. 'But if he is anything like his father, he will be a big baby.'

'You know for sure it's going to be a boy?'

'It's a boy, all right. My daughter-in-law is carrying her dummy pointing forward. It's definitely a boy.' She nodded with reinforced confidence. 'Everyone says so.'

'Big Mother is very lucky,' Mei said, glad to see a happy face.

'What can I do for you, my child?' asked the smiling woman.

'Where can one get a bite to eat around here?'

'There are some night cafés two blocks up. But not all of them clean, know what I mean? Go to my daughter-in-law's place, called *Lai Chun* – Coming of Spring.'

The woman put her knitting in a basket and got up from her chair. She was small and she moved with quick hands and light feet. This was a woman who liked to work, and work had kept her looking youthful.

'My son is at the restaurant helping out. Could you take a word to him for me? His name is Lao Da. Tell him that I'm getting tired. He should come back and shut the reception for the night.'

'Is this your son's hotel?'

'Goodness, no. We haven't that kind of money. It belongs to my cousin, his second uncle. My son is just looking after it, helping to manage the place, so to speak. It's a good deal. We get to come to Beijing and we have a room here for free. Lai Chun is theirs, a nice little business. My daughter-in-law is a very good cook. They call her Won Ton Queen. She used to help my son here, doing the cleaning. Now she runs the restaurant. An able woman, that daughter-in-law of mine is. When it's not busy here, my son goes over to help her. They're trying to pay back their debts as quickly as they can, and eventually buy his second uncle out.'

The woman stood under the single yellow light and pointed the way. Mei thanked her and stepped again into the darkness.

Further down the street, Mei found herself on the corner of a dirty alley, just as the old woman had described. It was like another world. The alley smelled of both urine and food. On the right it was dark, walled in by small huts with tar roofs. At the base of the wall were piles of dirt, loose bricks, trash and scrap metal from old woks or bicycles. Similar huts lined the left side of the alley, but these were front-facing, brightly lit and noisy. They were the night cafés where most hotel guests came to spend their evenings.

Mei walked through the yellow glow that leaked out from the windows. Her shadow on the wall was long and bent. Most of the windows were steamed up, obscuring the figures moving inside.

One of the doors opened. A young man carried out a basin of dirty water and dumped it by the wall. He stared at Mei long enough to make her uncomfortable.

Lai Chun was near the bottom of the alley. It was a small but airy place, with white plastic tables and plastic chairs. There were about a dozen customers, eating noisily from large soup bowls. A young man with quick feet shuttled between the tables and the kitchen, which was concealed behind a floral curtain. He had the same happy expression as the old woman at the guesthouse.

'Boss, soy sauce!' one of the customers called out.

Almost running, the young man delivered the sauce bottle, leaving it on the table and turning to Mei. 'Sorry, we haven't a free table, five minutes, please wait, I will get you a table in five minutes.' He talked fast, too.

'I'm all right. Your mother wanted me to give you a word,' Mei said.

'My mother?' He stopped buzzing.

'She said she's tired and that you can go back and shut the reception. Nothing is happening.'

My mother? questioned his eyes. They were bright and cheerful.

'Yes, your mother. Aren't you Lao Da? I've just come from the guesthouse.'

He laughed as if something had just clicked. 'Yes,' he said. 'My mother wants me to shut the reception. Thanks.'

He hurried back to the kitchen, sweeping up empty bowls and dirty chopsticks as he went.

After he had left, the curtain to the kitchen parted and a heavily pregnant woman came out, drying her hands on her apron. She greeted the regulars with 'Old Huang' or 'Uncle Ma'.

'Won Ton Queen, take a break,' they told her.

She gleamed. 'I'm fine. Eat slowly.' She bowed at her customers as she passed them.

She brought over a chair for Mei. 'Thanks, Big Sister, for the message. Lao Da usually drops back to check on Ma, but we have been busy tonight. The rush is finished now, though. These are the people who just got in on the night train, no more. Do you mind sitting here? Let me make you some of my special won ton.'

'That'd be good. I'm famished.' Mei smiled.

'Good.' She slapped her hands together. Her cheeks were blotched with brown pregnancy spots, yet Mei found it hard to imagine a face more pleasing.

The won ton was divine. The wrappings were made from paper-thin egg sheets and hand-rolled over fillings of fresh meat and seafood. They melted in her mouth. The soup base was so flavoursome, it must have come from bones that had been boiled patiently for days over a slow fire.

Lao Da returned and went into the kitchen. Won Ton Queen came to sit by Mei, asking her how she liked the dish. In the background, the regulars were drinking rice wine and chatting.

'Delicious, the best I've had,' said Mei.

That seemed to please Won Ton Queen.

'Fine,' she said. 'Come often, I will put a bit more in your bowl.' She moved her chair closer, leaning over Mei like a big sister chatting in a fruit market. 'I know it's not my business, but we don't have many young women come in here, especially not on their own. Sometimes, yes – but you don't look the type . . .'

'No, I haven't run away from home, and no, I am not married . . .' Mei shook her head. 'But you're right; I've come here for a reason. I'm looking for a man called Zhang Hong, a tough-looking man with a lot of muscle and a scar over his left eye. You see, his wife is a distant relative. They live in Luoyang. She is worried because he hasn't come home. He was in Beijing to sell an antique and was then supposed to take the money back.'

'How long has he been gone?'

'Over two weeks.'

'Maybe his business is not done yet?'

'It's finished. He's got the money.'

'I see. Well, I'm in the kitchen a lot. But if this Zhang Hong had been around, my regulars would know. Wait here.' She put one hand on the table and the other on the chair and pushed herself up. She wobbled over to see her regular customers.

Soon, she waved Mei across.

'You may want to look in Luck Come Together. Those who have money go there, don't they?' The person speaking was called Uncle Ma. He was an alert, beady-eyed little man in his later years.

Old Huang, oily-faced, interrupted. 'Luck Come Together is expensive, but always packed in the evening, though I honestly don't know why. Well, I suppose I know why. It's the only night-time entertainment centre around here. There is the karaoke machine and, of course, those hostesses. You'd think the poor bastards from the provinces couldn't afford to go there. But every night, they fill up the place like it was the last night of their lives.'

'Some local folks go there too,' Uncle Ma added, glancing at his friend across the table. 'You know the type, perverts and thugs.'

Old Huang shrugged. 'Drinks are expensive there, but a lonely traveller could get some action, get close to a woman's flesh. And if he has money, play a round of poker. He may get lucky too. Gambling is wrong and illegal. This is the Party's policy and I say a correct one. But a little bit now and then doesn't hurt anyone. Old Ma and I sometimes go to Luck Come Together to play a round of *Ma-jiang* – thirty, forty yuan, just for fun. Sometimes we win a small hand. But we are not addicted. If you are addicted, then gambling is a killer. *Ma-jiang* is different. It's a sophisticated game, not so dependent on luck.'

'Would you mind taking me to Luck Come Together?' asked Mei, smiling. Her big eyes flickered like fireflies on a summer's night. 'You see, Zhang Hong has been seen going around with a young woman friend. His wife wants him home before the money is all gone.'

'Well, if he is the gambling type, nothing's going to stop that,' Old Huang said, with a cunning look. He seemed pleased to be needed by a pretty young lady. He turned to his friend. 'Do you want to go? If your wife finds out . . .'

'Yes,' said Uncle Ma quickly, his head lowered and his little eyes casting an embarrassed glance at the table where his hands rested and where the tea had gone cold in its cup. 'I'll come too.'

18

The three of them set off for Luck Come Together.

It was a place of shadows, the only illumination the red lights over the tables. There was a smell of boiled rice wine. At a table to Mei's left, four men were taking bets on how much they could drink. Saltwater peanuts and empty beer bottles littered the table. To the right, two men were throwing their fists around, singing drinking songs and laughing. They wanted their lady companions to join in, but the women merely giggled and shook their heads like rattles. Behind the bar, two waitresses were whispering and exchanging meaningful glances with each other. They seemed to be talking about the man drinking alone in the corner.

At the large table in the middle of the room there was a group of local youths. They all smoked and drank and shared the same tough expressions. One of them was a girl, either the leader's girl or the leader herself. With the exception of one handsome boy, they all acted carefully around her, showing plenty of respect.

The manager greeted Old Huang and Uncle Ma warmly. He inquired about Mrs Ma, happiness and the weather for the next day. He indicated an empty table in the corner. Old Huang whispered something in his ear, to which the manager nodded and said, 'Of course, go straight in.'

They walked past the kitchen. Two cooks were sitting in front of plates of chopped white chicken and stir-fry greens, having a late dinner. They barely blinked when Mei and her escorts went by. Empty woks covered in months' worth of cooking grease lay idly on cold stoves. Opened cardboard boxes and half-drained sauce bottles were strewn around. A headless chicken lay on a wooden chopping board next to a massive steel knife.

Beyond the kitchen lay a gambling room. Halogen tubes burned above the smoke, and the air was pungent with the sour smell of beer. The ceiling was low and the floor cold, yet no one seemed troubled. There was an atmosphere of calm, as in an opium den where the customers were on their third pipes.

Gambling was these people's opium. By day they could have any of a number of occupations – they could be schoolteachers or well-off government employees. Or you might find a sweet grandmother with false teeth or a father who never allowed his children a thread of freedom. Some probably told lies – saying they were visiting neighbours, getting together with friends. Some had not been able to escape the reproaches of hysterical wives or enraged husbands, and sat at their tables full of shame and despair. But more likely they carried expressions of liberation and relief. These were the travellers who had come thousands of miles from home. In this big anonymous city they were out of reach of anyone they knew, and could really let loose.

'Hey, neighbours, another try at *Ma-jiang*?' A short man in his mid-fifties greeted them in a way that didn't pretend to be pleasant. He glanced at Mei suspiciously. His belly looked like a spare tyre.

'That's Lao Xia,' whispered Uncle Ma. 'He looks after the gaming tables.'

Old Huang took out a half-empty pack of Marlboros and jerked it open so that the cigarettes lined up neatly with their butts sticking out. Lao Xia pulled one from the pack. Old Huang lit it.

'No worries, she's a friend of Won Ton Queen,' said Old Huang, putting the packet back into his pocket. Mei remembered that Old Huang had been smoking a cheaper local brand in the café.

'Big stakes?' Old Huang pointed at the poker tables with his chin.

Old Xia puffed his Marlboro but made no reply. He glanced at the tables and the people around them, his serious expression seeming to suggest something important was going on.

There were three tables, each with four people clustered around them. At one of the tables, two uniformed policemen were being well looked after by a big-breasted hostess. Zhang Hong was not amongst the players.

At one of the *Ma-jiang* tables, a woman suddenly exclaimed 'full house', pushing over her wall of tiles. She stood up, glowing with excitement, grabbing the sheets of money she had won. She was about forty-five, a meaty woman with a tiny frame. Her lips were thin, the upper thinner and wider than the lower. A pair of fat eyelids had crushed her eyes into fine lines, which made her look as if she was squinting all the time. Her tight top hugged a pair of large melon breasts.

Uncle Ma leaned over. 'Madam Xia wins again.'

Madam Xia's partners seemed discouraged. They got up to

leave, looking as gloomy as if they had just lost their livelihoods.

'Old Huang, Old Ma!' Madam Xia called out, waving her hands.

The three of them went over to the square *Ma-jiang* table. Old Huang and Uncle Ma took their seats. Madam Xia looked at Mei and the empty chair next to her.

'You play?' she asked.

'No,' said Mei slowly. It was not entirely true. She had played before, in the Ministry. But she had always hated the game.

'Not enough to play for money,' she added.

'That's okay, we don't play stakes the first round,' said Madam Xia, who had already started to wash the tiles. 'Sit down. My husband doesn't like my playing here. He is worried about money. I don't really care about money. I come to play *Ma-jiang* and that's all.'

Her sausage fingers moved as calmly as if she was doing household chores. 'So how do you know these two pigs?'

'From Lai Chun,' replied Old Huang, smoking one of his cheap cigarettes.

Madam Xia started to build her wall of tiles. Looking at Mei sidelong, she asked, 'You are a Beijinger, aren't you? What were you doing at Lai Chun?'

Mei took her time, lining up her tiles carefully. When she had finished, she looked up and saw that Madam Xia was waiting for an answer.

'I came to look for someone and got friendly with Won Ton Queen,' said Mei.

'She's looking for a man from Luoyang called Zhang Hong,' Old Huang said angrily. 'The bastard came to Beijing to sell old stuff—'

'Antiques,' interrupted Uncle Ma, almost inaudibly, then hastily retreated into his own shadow.

'Whatever. So hear this, the guy gets the money, a lot of money. But he doesn't go home to his wife. Instead, he picks up a young girl and lives the high life in Beijing.' Old Huang blew some smoke and dumped a tile on the table. Mei picked it up.

'Ah, one of those again. Men – how can you trust them?' Madam Xia combed the wall of tiles in front of her with searching eyes. Across the table, Uncle Ma had buried his head in his tiles like a child in a candy store.

'What does this Zhang Hong look like?' Madam Xia asked, taking a new tile.

'He has a scar over his left eye, medium height, broad build.' Mei was keeping to the facts.

Madam Xia nodded. 'I don't think I've seen him here, but then, I don't come every day. And of course my husband never tells me anything. He is very discreet. But I find out things nonetheless.' She looked at Mei. 'You see, the hostesses know a lot around here. Let me ask my regular girl, Liu Lili. She's one of the hostesses for the gambling room. But I haven't seen her tonight.'

Nothing more was said. They played *Ma-jiang*, taking turns to change their tile holdings.

'How much money are we talking about? Ten, twenty thousand yuan?' Finally Madam Xia asked the question that was burning a hole in her heart.

'Much more,' said Mei.

'Heavens!' exclaimed Madam Xia, tapping the table with a tile.

'Enough to buy one of those hostesses,' Old Huang remarked with a smirk.

Madam Xia gave him a sharp glance, which made no impression. Old Huang merely grinned, caressing a tile in his hands as though to smother it. Uncle Ma sniggered.

'Let's get some tea.' Madam Xia waved to her husband. He came over to their table and then left the gambling room.

Madam Xia looked at Mei, smiling, and in a practised sweet-pea voice asked, 'So what is this antique that can fetch such money?'

'Something very old. I was told it was from the Han Dynasty.'

'Got to be older than Ming,' Old Huang said knowledgeably, speaking as if he were a true expert. 'We don't have anything like that in Beijing anymore. It was all smashed up in the Cultural Revolution. These days you can only find such things in the countryside.'

'I wonder.' Madam Xia had stopped moving the tiles. 'Big Wife Li from the second floor brought back antiques when she went to visit people she'd known from her labour camp time. I don't know whether she sold them. Ah, more than twenty thousand yuan, you say? I've got relatives in my hometown, a small village down south. I wonder whether they have anything like that.'

She tilted her head to one side as if it were being weighed down by the sheer magnitude of her thoughts. 'How would you know that they are genuine? Where would you go to sell them?'

'The stores in Liulichang buy them,' said Mei.

She could sense Madam Xia's enterprising mind taking wings. These days everyone was enterprising. A bit of gambling, a bit of buying and selling at the local stock-trading outpost, and a visit to poor relatives in hope of finding valuable antiques – it was all in a day's work.

A tea girl brought in a brown porcelain teapot and a stack of plastic teacups. She poured tea for everyone.

'Where's Lili?' Madam Xia asked.

'She hasn't been at work for a few days,' the tea girl replied. She had a long chin and her face was without expression, her gaze squinting, her short black hair parted in the middle. She was very young, sixteen or seventeen.

Some sort of scuffle had broken out at one of the poker tables. A beer bottle was smashed. Someone screamed, 'Fuck your mother!'

Everyone suddenly stopped moving. The two policemen stood up. Old Xia, stony-faced, marched over with stiff fists. He looked as if he could be cruel when he was angry.

Mei picked up her handbag from under the table and said that she was going to the toilet. No one seemed to hear, or care. She left through the kitchen. The two cooks had disappeared.

She found the cross-eyed tea girl in the front room. The lights seemed to have lost power. The same groups of drunks hovered over the same tables and hostesses, their singing now distorted by alcohol.

The tea girl was sitting on a chair chewing her fingernails and staring at nothing.

'There's a fight inside,' Mei said, leaning against the counter.

The tea girl glanced sideways at Mei and said nothing.

'You've worked here for a long time?'

'Two years,' the girl said reluctantly.

'Don't you want to be a hostess?'

The girl threw her a fierce look. 'What's your business?'

'Nothing. I just thought it would be better money.'

'I'm not allowed to drink with customers. Can't you tell that I have an unlucky face? I don't care for that kind of money anyway, not clean.'

'What about Lili? Does she care for the money?' Mei sat down on an empty chair next to the girl.

'Oh, yes,' she said. A dark shadow drifted almost imperceptibly across her face. 'She loves it.'

'Is that why she went off with Zhang Hong?'

The tea girl stopped fidgeting with her nails. 'Are you a cop?'

'No,' said Mei.

The girl stared. She seemed to be wondering whether she should believe Mei. She stretched her chin out absently.

Slowly Mei counted out three one-hundred yuan bills and folded them into a roll. She watched the girl staring at her fingers.

'Where can I find her?'

The tea girl took the money.

'Lili lives with her parents. Number six Wutan Hutong, off Exhibition Hall Road. She hates it, is always trying to make enough money to move out.'

Mei wrote down the address in her notebook. She thanked the tea girl and got up to go.

'Miss?' Mei turned and saw the girl standing against the counter, one hand holding the money inside her trouser pocket.

'She will come back, you'll see,' she said. 'She always does.'

Mei waited, but the tea girl said nothing more. Instead she turned away, gazing again at nothing.

19

The wind had picked up. Mei put the collar of her jacket up. The street lamps had been switched off and the wires overhead reached into darkness. Mei stepped silently through the narrow alleyways, past abandoned buildings, derelict huts and the occasional dimly lit window. The city was sleeping. She came to Lotus Pond Road and saw the lights of the train station ahead.

Inside her car, she took out the city map and pored over the *hutongs* off Exhibition Hall Road, looking for Wutan Hutong.

When she found it, she turned the key in the ignition. The Mitsubishi shivered, its engine hummed. Mei put the headlights on. It was ten to one in the morning. She turned out of the car park and onto Lotus Pond Road.

She went north at White Cloud Street and drove for a mile by stocky chestnut trees and anonymous grey apartment buildings. She crossed the City Moat and onto the west extension of the Boulevard of Eternal Peace. She took in a long breath and repeated the words silently – eternal peace. What a beautiful wish, and a fitting name for the road that led to the Forbidden

City. She thought about the golden dynasties of the past. In the dead of night, she was racing down the lonely streets of the northern capital of Kublai Khan in her little red Mitsubishi, and somewhere behind her she thought she heard the ghost of time.

Twenty minutes later, Mei turned off at Exhibition Hall Road and then into a one-lane street that swerved before becoming an unlit dirt path. Slowly the path narrowed until it was flanked by low courtyard houses and their belongings, and she could go no further. She switched off the engine and stepped out.

The oval spot of her torch moved like a magnifying glass, revealing tiny pebbles, candy wrappings and shreds of plastic and paper. A patch of vomit, pale and still moist, was piled at the side of a house to her left. Next to it was an old chest, unwanted belongings spilling out of it, and two rusty bicycles. A pair of white socks waved on the washing line above like flags admitting defeat.

Mei found no. 6, recently but carelessly repainted. With wind and rain, the double wooden door had shrunk in size and was chipped at the edges. Mei switched off her torch and slowly pushed the door open. It creaked like a thirsty man crying for water.

The courtyard was dark except for a pale yellow window in the west house. There was no sound or movement in any of the households. The light must have been left on for someone who was still expected to come home.

Mei backed out quietly, leaving the door ajar. She didn't know whether Lili's family lived in the west house, but something told her to wait. A daughter, however wayward, is seldom allowed to stay out overnight.

She moved her car out of the narrow path, stopped a few shadows down from the entrance to Wutan Hutong, and switched off the engine. Slowly her eyes began to adjust. She was able to make out certain shapes around her – a metre-high storage hut undoubtedly built without permission, a tar sheet that had been blown off the roof, and lifeless trees. A gust of wind sent a sheet of newspaper swirling into the alleyway.

Mei thought of her mother, lying inside the white space of the hospital. She wondered how she was in the night and whether pain had kept her awake. She tried to see her mother's face but instead saw her moving actively about her apartment the last time Mei had visited her. Mama had cooked fish. Later they had quarrelled.

'I'm sorry,' said Mei silently. But Mama was too far away to hear her.

A taxi pulled in to the street, stopping some distance away. The driver turned off the engine but left the lights on, outlining two figures, one taller than the other, as they walked from the car. Their shadows stretched into the night.

It was a man and a woman. Mei watched them walking unsteadily into the dark *hutong*.

Something metallic, perhaps a bicycle, fell over, echoing in the silence. Then there was another faint bang, further away. Mei waited, her eyes and mind awake.

A few minutes later, the man came out of the *hutong*, stumbling into the blinding headlights. His shadow elongated and turned into a monster with a tiny head.

Then he disappeared. The engine started. Its headlights shook, accelerating towards Mei's car. She ducked her head beneath the dashboard.

The taxi swung into the *hutong* and made a left turn towards the main road. Mei waited for it to get a little distance ahead then followed it out, headlights off.

Once on Exhibition Hall Road, Mei turned her lights on. The taxi drove southwards and then east to Glory City Gate, where it took a circle under the flyover into a lay-by. There was a light at the entry to a brand-new hotel. The opening banner was still hanging over the entrance: Celebrating the Opening of Hotel Splendour.

The taxi turned into the hotel's driveway. Mei stopped her car on the kerb and killed the lights. She watched the back of the man disappearing into the hotel, swaying from side to side. A minute later, the taxi started off again, headlights blazing, back to the road of wanderers and dreamers.

Mei drove home, happy in the knowledge that she could come back tomorrow morning and find Zhang Hong.

20

'I am here to see Zhang Hong,' Mei told the reception clerk at the Hotel Splendour. She looked at her watch. It was coming up to eleven o'clock.

'Room 402.' He smiled eagerly, showing neat white teeth.

'That *is* service. You didn't even need to look it up.' Mei was impressed.

The young clerk blushed, lowering his eyes. Rather attractive, Mei thought.

'Miss exaggerates. I wish I were that good. No, I only remember the room because I looked him up for someone a short while ago.'

That someone could not have been Lili. She would have gone straight up to his room.

'When was that?'

'Ten, maybe fifteen, minutes ago.'

Someone called for him. 'Excuse me,' he said. At the other end of the reception desk, a couple was disputing something. The woman pointed and waved her hands.

Mei left the reception and went down a carpeted corridor.

It was brightly lit and smelled of new paint. Mei pushed the call button and listened for the lift. It creaked from somewhere inside the wall and finally halted with a judder. Mei stepped in.

Mei cast her eyes over the numbers on the doors in the new-looking fourth-floor corridor.

Suddenly she heard hurried footsteps. Mei stopped. A figure came around the corner and rushed past her. She whirled around in time to see a man's back disappearing down the stairs.

Mei ran. The door of room 402 was ajar.

A slight breeze entered through a half-opened window, moving a thin white curtain. The room had been ransacked. A floral duvet, pillows and pieces of men's clothing were dumped on the floor. A suitcase had been turned inside out. One of the bedside lamps had fallen to the ground. The mattress had been turned around and was hanging off the bed.

An expensive bottle of *Wu Liang Ye* rice wine – Five Virtuous Liquid – lay on the floor and the room stank of its spilled contents. A porcelain shot cup had rolled to the window, where it was resting on its side.

A stiff body in a new tracksuit lay on the floor. Mei gasped at the sight of his face. It was frozen in a flinching grimace. Blood had trickled from his nose and mouth. The scar above his eye, less bluish than the rest, gawked at her as if it were alive.

She covered her mouth. Her breath shortened. Suddenly she couldn't find air. Her hands trembled and her body shook. She backed away, hitting the wall.

A faint roar of a motorbike passed somewhere in the distance. Spring sunshine filtered through the white curtain.

Mei stared at the scarred face. She had finally found Zhang Hong, but he was not going to answer any of her questions.

Lying dead in twisted agony, he looked small and helpless. Mei wondered what he had done to deserve such a death.

Mei drew a couple of big breaths and walked over. She squatted next to the body and touched its face. It was stone cold.

She stood up. She thought about the two shadows walking away from the yellow headlights at Wutan Hutong. She thought also, oddly, of the Luoyang peony, the national flower, with its baroque petals and soft colours of yellow, pink and white. She had never been to Luoyang. She couldn't think of anything else belonging to the city. Zhang Hong was the first person who had linked her to it, far away to the west. Did he have a family there? Were they still waiting for his return? Mei felt her heart sinking.

She walked over to the bathroom. Whoever had searched the place had done a thorough job; everything had been tossed on the floor. She found a leather toiletry bag, toothbrush, towels, soap, toothpaste, a bull-horn comb, a strip of condoms and a bottle of Five Flower Oil for cuts and bruises.

Mei wondered what the person had been searching for.

She took a last look at the dead man and backed out, closing the door behind her. Quiet reigned in the corridor.

In the lobby it was noisy. A group of five men with red alcoholic eyes had just come in with their shopping bags. They had obviously had a good lunch. A young woman with grasshopper legs and a short skirt tapped her heels by the door, possibly waiting for someone. The argumentative couple was still at it, the man now waving his hands.

Mei went up to the young clerk at the reception desk and said, 'You'd better call the police.'

'Police?'

'Yes. He's dead.'

'Who?'

'The man in room 402, Zhang Hong.'

It took another ten seconds for his smile to evaporate. Then he jumped to the telephone. Other reception clerks hurried across. Heads started to turn, voices rose. Mei gave one of them her business card and suggested he pass it on to the police.

The manager was called. Guests hovered around the reception area wanting to know what had happened.

Mei left quietly. She had to find Lili – fast.

21

On Glory City Gate Boulevard, Mei began to feel sick. She pulled over to a side street and vomited. Droves of high school kids in white tracksuits with red piping were on their way home for lunch. They frowned at Mei. There was a small vending hut at the street corner. Mei went over. A cardboard sign at the end of the counter read: Telephone, three yuan per minute. Two girls in tracksuits stopped to buy sweets. They carried on their conversation with an air of self-importance, rolling their eyes, laughing and locking arms as though they would be friends for life. Mei bought a bottle of Coca-Cola and downed it in one go. The drink helped to settle her nausea. After a few minutes, she was able to get back in the car and drive on.

She walked down the narrow alley of Wutan Hutong. In daylight, it was overcrowded with life. Grandmothers chatted with each other while hanging up washing. Their conversations stopped when Mei passed by in her high heels. A woman who looked about one hundred years old sat on a wooden stool by the wall, alone and smiling. Two old men were locked in a battle of Go by the gate of a courtyard house. Three toddlers in open-bottomed pants played with dirt and ants that lived under the dried-up trees, paying Mei no attention. Wild red flowers bloomed unnoticed atop decaying tile roofs.

No. 6 was made up of three low-beamed houses surrounding a courtyard, forming the shape of a U. Once this would have been a single-family dwelling. Now three families lived here. The middle house, facing the entrance, was the biggest and, traditionally, would have been the main reception room. The west and east houses were smaller; they would have been bedrooms.

In the middle of the courtyard stood an old brown tree. A family of magpies had made a nest amongst its bare branches. Under the tree, a middle-aged man with black-rimmed glasses sat on a tiny wooden stool with a basin of water. Next to the washing basin there was a beaten-up bicycle standing upside down. The man held a pink tube under the water and searched for the puncture.

'Who are you looking for?' he questioned Mei.

'Liu Lili.'

For almost a minute, the man stared at Mei from behind his glasses. Finally, he pointed at the west house and spat.

Mei thanked him and went up to the door. She knocked on it a few times, rattling the narrow wooden frame. After about two minutes, a soft voice rose from the inside. 'Who are you?'

Mei heard footsteps stopping at the door.

'My name is Wang Mei. I'd like to talk to you.'

There was no reply. She tried again: 'It's very important, about Zhang Hong.'

At the window, floral curtains parted about an inch. A pair of eyes appeared. Mei smiled. Twenty seconds later, the door opened.

The first thing Mei noticed was the smell, unmistakably bitter and with enough kick to upset the neighbourhood. It was a smell that Mei was familiar with – perhaps even fond of. It reminded her of the dark winter days of childhood. As a child, Mei was rather sickly, and her mother frequently took her to see Chinese herbalists.

'Are you sick?' asked Mei.

Lili sat down next to a square dining table covered with a white embroidered tablecloth. She wore a man's woollen vest over a skimpy little black dress. She had a permed bob with a thick fringe above her round eyes. With her puffy cheeks and pouting lips she had the look of a child, but Mei couldn't tell her exact age.

Lili glanced at the clay pot brewing on the stove. 'A minor illness,' she said.

Black smoke billowed from the stove, drifting along the wall and out through a hole cut in the boarded-up window.

'I know a very good doctor at the Chinese Medicine Research Institute, if you need another opinion,' said Mei. Chinese herbalists were notorious for rarely agreeing with each other.

The lights in Lili's eyes were soft, as was her voice. 'Please sit down. Did Zhang Hong tell you about me?' She was neither nervous nor eager. She combed her hair with her fingers.

'No. He didn't tell me anything. Are you in love with him?'

Lili burst out laughing. 'Don't you know that he's the same age as my father?'

'But you like him.'

'I don't know. He's a gambler, as bad as they come. But he treats me well – I mean, with respect.'

She crossed one leg over the other, dangling a plastic slipper from her toes.

'How did you two meet?'

'Who are you anyway?' Lili tilted her head, slipping her pink fingers through her hair again.

Mei passed her a card, which Lili read two or three times. 'What is an information consultant?'

'People pay a fee for me to look for something or someone. For example, I was hired by a collector to look for an antique that Zhang Hong might have known about. No, it is not the Han Dynasty ceremonial bowl.'

'What did he say?'

'I didn't have a chance to ask him.'

Lili played with the card and smiled. 'He lost all the money he got from the Han bowl. Can you believe it?'

'He did what?' Mei was shocked.

'Oh, we went to play big stakes at an entertainment centre in West City District. He just had the most terrible luck. But not to worry, he told me yesterday that he'll soon be rich again.' Lili toyed with the plastic flowers in a vase on the table. 'When he was at Luck Come Together, he actually won sometimes. When he did, we'd go eat at expensive restaurants and then he'd take me shopping.'

The talk of gambling must have reminded her of something. She got up suddenly.

'Excuse me,' she said. She vanished through a blue curtain into what Mei guessed was her bedroom.

When Lili came back she had a packet of cigarettes and a lighter in her hands. She stopped by the stove and lifted the clay pot down with a poker. Then, with the same poker, she picked up a heavy iron lid and covered the stove. She poked and shifted the lid until it sat tightly on the stove's mouth. She then put the clay pot back on top.

'Can we go outside? I'm dying for a smoke,' she said. 'My parents won't let me smoke inside the house.'

Outside, she leaned against the doorframe and surrounded herself with smoke rings. 'Do you know what the medicine is for?' she asked suddenly.

Mei looked at Lili's face and wondered how old she was.

'It's for women's illness. I get terrible cramps when I have my period, so bad that I sometimes wish I were dead. It's a torture that never ends. This is why I am always off work for four, five days a month. No one bothers about it anymore.'

'Does the medicine work?'

'I hope so. This is my fifth dose. I think the pain is getting better, but I can't be sure. It makes me nauseous sometimes. The herbalist says it's to be expected.'

She looked over to the brown tree. 'See that man over there? He's been unemployed for a while. All day long he hangs about and spies on me.' She shot the man a hostile look and he quickly turned away.

'What are you looking at, you dirty old man!' she shouted at him. 'He thinks I am a slut,' she explained to Mei. She shouted again: 'At least I am not eating my wife's meal!'

'It's the money I am after, of course,' she said to Mei. 'Look at it here: no gas, no running water or central heating, no privacy. The house is full of worthless junk. I swear I'd never live like my parents. I go out with clients from Luck Come Together. We go to high-class restaurants and nightclubs.' She puffed brutally and exhaled through her perfectly formed rings of smoke.

'My parents think I'm a slut. The other hostesses at Luck Come Together think I'm a slut. As if they are any better. What's the difference between them and me? They let men buy them drinks and touch them.' Her eyes were wide open. She spoke with the conviction of a teenager who had just discovered the meaning of love. 'Why should I make money for the management?' Her childish voice lingered like those smoke rings, sending ripples through the air.

Mei let the question hang, waiting for the girl to go on. When she didn't, Mei said, 'You mentioned that Zhang Hong talked about becoming rich again. Did he tell you where the money was to come from?' The questions did not fit with the mood, but Mei needed some answers.

'What money?' Lili lowered her eyes. She had been gazing at the nest at the top of the tree. 'Are you spying on me?' She stared at Mei as if she had never seen her before.

Mei took a step back. Suddenly she saw something murky and sinister behind Lily's eyes, something that did not quite belong to that rosy-cheeked face of child-like innocence.

'Don't you worry, he'll be rich and he will share his money with me.' Lili leaned into Mei's face. 'The eye of jade,' she whispered.

She sniffed loudly, and began to sway. She twisted her index finger into her permed hair, like a drill. Her round eyes clouded. She giggled.

Mei wondered what the medicine was really for. Something wasn't quite right with the girl.

The bike man was now heating glue on a burner. A sharp odour rose from streaks of thin black smoke.

Quietly Mei walked out of the courtyard and into the normality of noisy alleys and laundry lines.

22

From the car Mei made a call to her office. Gupin told her that Ms Fang had called from the Motor Vehicle Bureau. 'She asked you to call her back,' he said.

Fang Shuming sounded cautious on the phone. 'Could we meet up? It's better to talk face to face.'

Mei sensed that Shuming had found something for her. They agreed to meet after work in the street-centre park on Ten Thousand Springs Road.

In the park a bearded man was trying to fly a kite. He wet his index finger and held it in the wind. Then he ran with the kite, each time from a different angle. Mei watched the kite struggle from the pavilion.

On the street, traffic was roaring. People were on their way home for dinner. Jam-packed buses rocked past.

Mei thought of Zhang Hong. He must at one point have travelled on one of these buses. He might have passed street-centre parks like this one. Perhaps he had seen the Hotel Splendour from a bus, liked the look of it, and moved there after he got paid. But now he was a cold body lying in the morgue. Was he killed by the thugs from the gambling house? Had there been a struggle? Had he been poisoned? For what?

Mei thought about Lili, the girl with the mind of a fourteen-year-old and the body of a twenty-year-old. She seemed to have no idea how far she'd gone or where she belonged.

A young couple, unmistakably migrant workers, had sat down on one of the stone benches in the square. The girl laid her head in her boyfriend's lap. She looked exhausted. The tight jumper she was wearing rode up over her naked belly. He looked as if he had just come off work, perhaps from the kitchen of a hotel or a restaurant. Sometimes they kissed, not passionately, but painfully. Two local pensioners were taking their daily walk around the square, glancing spitefully at the young couple.

A few yards away, a sparrow skipped mindlessly along a stone path, looking for food. The wind had died a little and the air was growing colder. A distant fragrance of clove was infusing the dusk like a tiny drop of pigment in clear water.

A cacophonous beat of drums and cymbals burst in from the distance. Mei listened as the noise grew closer. A procession of *Yang Ge* dancers appeared – men and women of fifty or sixty years of age, in loud make-up. The dancers wore silk pants with wide legs and balloon-sleeved shirts. Their feet, in white socks and black canvas shoes, danced crazily. As they went forward, they tossed their heads and shook their red silk handkerchiefs about exuberantly. Their faces glowed with bliss.

Yang Ge was originally a popular peasants' dance, performed around bonfires in villages and fields. It was a dance of celebration that mimicked the blossoming flowers and the flapping of birds' wings. The People's Liberation Army brought *Yang Ge* into the grand cities. Later on, somewhere along that winding road of revolution, *Yang Ge* was transformed into an art form. But after Chairman Mao died, *Yang Ge* was kicked a thousand *li* back to the fields. The fashion in the cities was ballroom dancing, elegant and Western. Ling Bai and her neighbours took lessons at the Comrade Activity Centre. Mei did foxtrots at student canteens turned dance halls on Sunday evenings. Lu was one-half of the University League Ballroom Dance champion pair. Then last year, out of the blue, *Yang Ge* had been revived. No one knew how or by whom. All of a sudden Beijing had thousands of *Yang Ge* parades at dusk, organised by citizens themselves, causing traffic chaos.

Plenty of people had stopped to watch the *Yang Ge* dancers. Some people pointed and laughed. A group of teenagers in tracksuits, on their way home after a game of football, watched in silence, looking disgusted and horrified.

A plump woman pushing a spotless Flying Pigeon bicycle made her way to the pavilion. She was a woman who dressed with great care: her silk scarf had been chosen to match the colour of her jacket, and she wore leather court shoes that belonged to a woman ten years younger. She parked her bicycle next to the pavilion and came up the stone steps. Her permed hair hardly moved.

'I pass here every day, but I've never stopped,' Shuming said, smoothing down her blue woollen jacket. 'My goodness, you can see every dancing foot from up here!'

'Good to see you, Shuming. You look great.' Mei stood up to greet her friend. She had helped Shuming in her divorce.

'Oh, hardly. How can I? Too busy at work.' Shuming sat down. 'Do you know that every month there are ten thousand new licence plate applications in Beijing? There has to be a waiting list. We can't cope, and neither can Beijing's roads.'

She pulled out a tissue and wiped her nose, her cheeks flushed with warmth.

'But I do feel good, much better than when I was married to that disgrace. And I have you to thank for it.' She looked at Mei and smiled. 'At one point I had worried about being single again, but now I love it, so much freedom. I think divorce has done me good. It has taught me self-respect.'

She laughed, turning around to watch the *Yang Ge* dancers trotting their costumed selves in front of the pavilion.

'Look at that one, the fat lady who looks like me. Look at how her feet move! People have this ridiculous belief that fat people are slow and clumsy. It's not true. Some of us are very agile. You know why? Because we've got a lot of energy, naturally, from eating so much.' Shuming laughed a man's laugh.

'What was it that you couldn't tell me on the phone?' Mei asked Shuming.

'I've got the registration for the licence plate number you gave me. The Audi belongs to the Ministry for State Security.'

'The secret service?'

The Ministry for Public Security, where Mei used to work, was the headquarters of the police, the equivalent of Scotland Yard. The Ministry for State Security, however, was the true envy of all: the headquarters of the secret police and the intelligence service, the Chinese KGB.

Shuming lifted her eyebrows and nodded knowingly.

Mei was at a loss. Big Papa Wu was meeting someone from the secret service? Mei wondered who this antique dealer really was.

'Could you find out to whom the car was allocated?' asked Mei.

'Not from our system. The allocation of official cars is an internal matter for the Ministry.'

Mei was disappointed.

Shuming moved closer and lowered her voice. 'I don't know what kind of case you're on or what you are trying to do. But please be careful, Mei.' She stood up to go. 'Goodbye. If there is anything else you need, just call.'

She went down the stairs and soon her plump body and the Flying Pigeon had vanished from sight.

Mei made her way out of the street-centre park. The traffic had begun to ease on Ten Thousand Springs Road. A row of street lamps glittered like a pearl necklace. Smoke was rising from the chimneys of newly built restaurants. The aroma of fat sizzling in spicy brown sauce and sugar lingered in the air.

A mean-faced woman jumped up from her wooden stool as soon as she saw Mei entering the car park, which was empty aside from Mei's red Mitsubishi and a big blue tour bus.

'You said you were only going to leave your car here for a little while!' the woman snapped. She strode over, a large canvas army bag swinging at her hips. Her hands were brown and claw-like and streaked with prominent veins. She thrust one of them in Mei's face. 'Five yuan extra,' she said sternly.

'It's not like the car park is full!' Mei protested.

'Full or not, it's none of your business. I did you a favour.'

Mei pulled out a five-yuan note and slapped it into the woman's hand. She was too tired to argue.

23

Night had fallen by the time Mei reached home.

She called Little Auntie.

'Big Sister is more or less the same. Sometimes she is alert and clear. Sometimes she is confused. She hasn't eaten anything for three days now, so the doctor put in a feeding tube so that she can get some nutrition. A few people have come to visit her. In the morning, the director of Elderly Comrade Affairs came. He asked about her condition and saw the doctor. He said that the work unit would try their best to meet the medical costs. Then someone called Song Kaishan came. He said he was an old friend.'

'Did he see Mama?'

'Big Sister was awake so he talked to her for a while, maybe for ten minutes.'

'What did they talk about?'

'I don't know,' Little Auntie said. 'He wanted to be alone with her. Your Uncle Chen came in the afternoon. Big Sister was asleep, so we chatted a little bit. He said that he knew Mr Song.'

'Who is he anyway? Why is he suddenly coming to see Mama?'

'Oh, he is just an old friend,' Little Auntie said quickly. 'Are you well?'

'I suppose. I'm working on a case. It helps me to keep my mind off things.' Mei paused; she had just thought of something. 'Did Lu visit Mama? We agreed that she would go today.'

'She couldn't. She called to say that something important had come up.'

'Would you like me to come so that you can have a rest?'

'I don't need rest,' said Little Auntie. 'The worker-help does much of the night shift.'

After a few more minutes, they hung up.

Mei went to the bathroom, brushed her teeth, washed her face and dried it with a towel. She rubbed a generous dose of night cream on, then crawled under the feathery down duvet. All she wanted to do now was to curl up like a cat and go to sleep.

The traffic noise from the ring-road persisted. As usual, just when she was falling asleep, someone raced by on a motorbike.

She turned to lie on her side. The softness of the pillow embraced her, and after a while pulled her into a deep sleep.

Then her telephone rang.

How could that be? She was sure she had switched it off.

She got up and walked into the living room, where the phone was lying on the table next to the sofa.

'Hello?'

Nothing.

'Hello? Hello?'

No one.

'Who's there?' she shouted.

There was a click, followed by a long beep.

Something had happened to Mama! Mei panicked. She had to get to the hospital. Mei started to run but fell to her knees. Something had hit her over the head, a large bat. Then she heard a loud bang, then another and another. Mei opened her eyes, like a deer caught in headlights. She was sweating and her heart throbbing. The loud pounding did not stop. Someone was banging on her door.

Mei rolled over and turned on the light. The alarm clock read 23:55. She groaned, her feet searching for the plastic slippers she had kicked off two hours earlier.

'Who is it?' she asked.

She turned the lock and opened the door slightly. It was Big Sister Hui, angry-eyed, mouth wide open.

'Where have you been? I've been trying to call you for two days. Didn't you get my messages?'

'The answering machine's broken.'

'And what do you think you are doing?' Big Sister Hui stared at Mei's pyjamas.

'Sleeping.'

'But it's Friday night!'

Big Sister Hui was heavily made-up. Her eyebrows were drawn in. She wore peach blusher on her round cheeks, and red lipstick; the lipstick had smudged a little at the corners of her mouth. Her forehead glistened. She was wearing orange satin trousers and a mandarin-collared shirt that had red embroidery at the cuffs. The scent of her perfume washed over Mei like a wave.

'You must come with me straight away.' Big Sister Hui marched inside.

'Where?'

'Party.'

Mei closed the door and followed her friend into the living room.

'But I don't want to go to a party. I'm tired. I've had a tough couple of days.'

'Nonsense. You're coming. I promised Yaping that I'd bring you.'

Big Sister Hui deposited her maternal behind on the sofa.

'What are you talking about?' Mei's mind froze.

'Yaping is in Beijing on a business trip. All our old classmates are having a get-together at his hotel. He's divorced.'

Mei's throat tightened. She couldn't speak.

'Don't just stand there. Go, get ready.' Big Sister Hui took out a make-up kit and opened it. The palette ignited like a small powder bomb.

'Hurry up!' she barked.

Mei went into the bathroom. She felt dizzy. Thoughts swirled inside her head like a storm. 'Yaping is in Beijing.' Even as she repeated these words to herself, she still couldn't believe that it was true. It sounded like a joke. Maybe someone was playing with her mind. She looked around. Nothing was out of the ordinary. Her make-up lay scattered in a little basket by the sink; a pink soap lay inside the white porcelain dish. In the mirror, she caught sight of her face, freckled as it always was, though paler.

She washed her face with cold water. He had been gone for nine years. She had burned all his letters. She had tried to forget. It had not been easy. From time to time, he still returned to her thoughts. She had imagined meeting him one day, some day in the far future when they were both old and grey. She had imagined that when they met again she would be calm and forgiving. But then, without warning, he was back, single again. What had happened? Questions raced inside her head. Was he sad? Had he changed? Would he recognise her? Would she recognise him? What would they say to each other? Was there anything to say?

An overwhelming mix of emotions rose up inside her, like water rising from a deep well, her thoughts tangled up. One minute she didn't want to go. She felt hurt, humiliated. She didn't want him to see that she was still single and think that she still loved him. But when the minute passed, she longed to see him again, to hear his voice, even if just for a night.

Mei shook her head. She did her make-up, dressed and went out to the living room.

'What took you so long?' Big Sister Hui complained. 'Let's go. The car is waiting.'

They went downstairs. A black Mercedes-Benz was parked outside her building. The driver jumped out and opened the door for the ladies.

'Goodness gracious, what is this?' asked Mei, not believing her eyes. Big Sister Hui was a lecturer at Peking University. Her husband, an engineer, was no tycoon either.

'It's Yaping's. He sent it for you.'

24

From the back seat of the car, Mei watched the streets of Beijing passing. It was like a procession of the years. Street lamps approached, bringing with them mushrooms of yellow light, and then they vanished, leaving only dark shadows and lost secrets.

Like any other city, Beijing seemed more romantic at night. Newly erected business towers illuminated the skyline with wondrous expectations. The windows of run-down matchboxes were now lit up with the promise of love and affection. The last street vendors were shutting up, packing barrel stoves and wooden stools onto flatbed carts and pushing them with bent backs to the rat-infested tin rooms they shared with other migrant workers. Their faces lit up with the thought of warmth, beds and hometowns. Half-empty buses hummed nostalgically down narrow lanes. Night was like a magic brush, blacking out all the ugliness so that the hour of love and longing could unfold.

'I tried to call you earlier hoping you would come to dinner,' Big Sister Hui said to Mei. 'Everyone asked whether you were coming. Well, everyone except Yaping.'

Mei watched the yellow lights come and go. They were gathering speed.

'After dinner, some people left. They had a long bus-ride home or needed to pick up children from grandparents or whatever reason. At the end only five of us left for the VIP room. I could see that Yaping was getting nervous, like an ant on a hot stove. So I told him that I'd bring you in myself. He said, 'Take my driver.' I tell you, he puts up with us, but the only person he's interested in seeing is you.'

'You always exaggerate,' said Mei, unmoved. 'He married someone else, remember?'

Their car came off the ring-road. At the bottom of the exit, they were joined by other cars and a few bicycles.

'I knew that you'd come,' said Big Sister Hui. 'You just needed someone like me to give you a yank.'

Mei turned to look at her old friend, one moment a caked face with smudged lips, and another, with the street lamps abandoned behind them like used-up chopsticks, just a pair of glowing eyes.

Inside the Great Wall Sheraton Hotel, amber and white crystal lights cascaded down seven storeys to an atrium. Between two giant columns, glass lifts were rising like bright lanterns towards the ceiling. On the marble floor, cool as a mirror, a jazz band was playing. Businessmen in dark suits and casually dressed tourists sipped cocktails in lounge chairs.

Mei had the feeling that she was being stared at when Big Sister Hui led her into the hotel lobby. Despite having worn her best evening outfit, she felt out of place. Her purple round-necked cashmere tunic dress was not from the Lufthansa Centre, nor was it imported from Hong Kong or Japan or South Korea. It was from Wangfujing Department Store, where she knew she could get the best quality cashmere for the money she could afford. Unfortunately, the store had stopped updating their styles since 1982. She had never cared before, but suddenly Mei was painfully conscious of it.

Big Sister Hui guided her into the Passion Night Club. They passed through a disco in full swing, the space crowded with pleasure seekers. Laser lights blitzed the dance floor, freezing forms and faces in weird attitudes and expressions.

They walked on, the music fading behind them, leaving only a pounding beat. They turned a corner into a narrow hallway. A long carpet stretched into the distance.

They followed it to the end of the hall and the last door on the left.

The room reeked of tobacco and alcohol. Mei saw a group of figures. Two people cuddled on a sofa in the corner. A girl in a blue *Qi Pao* dress leaned over the karaoke machine, thigh-high side-slits revealing her white legs. A man was singing into a microphone. Another man held a beer bottle in one hand and conducted with the other.

'Look who's here!' shouted Big Sister Hui.

The conductor's hand remained in the air. The couple in the corner divided. The singer stopped singing and turned around. Two strands of hair, wet from sweat, fell over his forehead. His white shirt, opened two buttons from the top, showed a toned body.

His eyes met Mei's.

Yaping strode over, still holding the microphone. On the karaoke monitor the words of a love song were traced in silence.

'Hello,' he said.

Mei recalled the gentle voice that once, long ago, had touched her heart.

'Come and sit down.' He gave her his hand. 'Good to see you.'

Mei did not take his hand. Instead she walked over to the cream leather sofa, avoiding his gaze. Mei said hello to the conductor, who had sat down to drink beer and smoke. She greeted also, at length, the slender person in the corner and a spiky-haired teenager whom he had introduced as his girlfriend. Mei had not seen Liang Yi for years. He was still devastatingly handsome and still a playboy.

'Big Sister, I owe you one.' Yaping turned to Big Sister Hui with a smile. 'What would you like to drink? More food?'

Before she could respond, he had turned to the girl who had been operating the karaoke machine. 'Miss, could we please have another fruit platter and some of your house special duck tongue? And more beer and wine.'

The waitress wiggled her tiny waist and left.

Suddenly a side door swung open and Guang's thundering voice came out of the toilet. 'His mother's, it won't come off!' His chest was soaking wet. He was holding a white shirt that had turned pink. He glared at the room. 'Why so quiet? Who's not singing?' he hollered. His face and eyes were red.

'Oh, Guang, you're drunk!' screamed Big Sister Hui.

'No. I just smell like one,' he laughed, waving a finger at her.

When he saw Mei, he stumbled over, bones cracking. 'Mei, you don't give my brother face. You don't come, after thousands and hundreds of calls. Still got your nose high in the air?'

Yaping put a hand on his shoulder. 'Cool it,' he said quietly.

Guang waved at him as if to say, 'I know.' He stretched his long legs, breathing sadly.

'Hey, I've missed the fun here,' exclaimed Big Sister Hui. 'Who wants to sing with me? Guang, you and me, a duet!'

At this suggestion, Guang cheered up. They went over to the machine to choose a song.

Two waitresses brought in more food and drinks: bowls of nuts, melons, pineapples, strawberries and plates of cold cuts. The waitresses wore identical royal-blue *Qi Po* and identical broad smiles. One was tall, long-haired and beautiful. The other was ordinary-looking, with short hair.

'Still don't drink beer?' Yaping said with a smile, sitting down next to Mei. She could almost touch his warm breath. His face had changed very little, but its expressions had matured.

'Still don't,' said Mei, returning his smile.

The ice was broken.

Big Sister Hui and Guang were old singing partners who used to represent their department in competitions. Nine years on they could still sing in harmony.

Yaping poured a glass of red wine for Mei. 'Hope you like it. The wine selection here is rather poor.' He apologised as though it was his fault that he could not offer her something better.

Mei took a sip and put the glass down. She wasn't a wine drinker either.

'I was surprised to hear that you are now a private detective.'

'Why? I can't be a detective?' asked Mei, her eyes flickering.

'No, I don't mean it as a criticism. In some ways I'm sure you make a very good detective, clever and extremely rational. But I just don't think of you as someone who is interested in other people's lives. At school you were never really part of the class or involved with what was going on around you. A lot of people thought you were arrogant. I thought of you as isolated but content to be so. Is that fair?'

Mei shrugged.

'What made you decide to become a private eye?' Yaping picked a few cold cuts for her plate.

'It seemed to be the natural thing to do. I had been involved with police work. When I left the Ministry I thought I'd try doing it privately.'

'Why did you leave the Ministry?'

'It's a long story and I don't feel like telling it, okay?'

'I understand,' said Yaping.

The red wine and the marinated duck tongues mingled, sharp and appetising. Yaping moved closer. 'Why don't you tell me more about your work. What do you do? Tap people?'

Mei laughed. 'No, tapping is illegal. But then, so is having a detective agency. We get around somehow. I do tail people sometimes. I also use camcorders and cameras.'

'Aha, photography. I remember. You liked to photograph nature. But your mother wasn't happy about it. She'd rather you interacted more with people.'

The mention of her mother, like a stone tossed into calm water, disturbed her peace. Suddenly she heard Guang. He had his arm around the waist of the plain-looking waitress and was singing his heart out. Left on the sofa, his beeper sounded, not for the first time. His wife must be getting annoyed. Big Sister Hui was now having a passionate discussion with the conductor. The playboy and his girlfriend went back to kissing and pawing at each other's bodies.

Yaping didn't notice the change in Mei's mood. 'Remember those trips we used to make to the mountains to photograph wildlife? You were so excited, you hardly noticed me. And those picnics we had. We filled our travelling aluminium tins with fizzy juice-water. There was no juice in that stuff at all, was there? Pure toxic chemicals. But how I miss the taste of it. I have looked for it since I have been back but they don't seem to make it anymore.'

The tea arrived, but Mei had lost her appetite.

'I'm sorry, I have to go home,' she said sadly. She felt loneliness suddenly weighing on her. 'My mother's in the hospital. I need to go see her in the morning.'

'What's wrong?'

'She's had a stroke. The doctor says she may not recover.'

'I am so sorry. I didn't know.'

'I'd love to stay and catch up, but . . .' she lowered her long eyelashes. Life was full of difficult choices.

'Let me take you home,' said Yaping, standing up.

'No. You can't desert all these friends. They've come especially to see you.'

'Then take my car. My driver can drop you off.'

He gave her his hand, which she took. Looking into his eyes, she felt the strength ebbing from her body. The touch of his skin was warm and inviting.

'Are you leaving already?' Big Sister Hui and the conductor stood up.

'Mei's mother is very ill. She needs to go to the hospital in the morning,' Yaping explained.

The playboy and his body extension paused in their embrace for long enough to say goodbye. Guang was beyond redemption, clutching the waitress, singing and crying.

Yaping asked the long-haired waitress to tell his driver to bring the car around. Informing his friends that he would be back soon, he picked up Mei's coat, and they walked out.

The disco had closed, the crowd gone, and the hallway was empty. They walked side by side.

'I am going back to America tomorrow evening. Can I see you again?'

'I don't know.'

'Let me drive you to the hospital tomorrow.'

'I have a car.'

They walked quietly for a while, then reached the atrium. Mei's heels clicked on the marble floor. The glass lifts were anchored at ground level. The empty space remained lit up like a crystal palace.

'I want to explain to you why I got married,' said Yaping finally. He was careful in the way he said it. It sounded like he had rehearsed the line many times before. Mei heard the words panting inside his throat.

'There's nothing to explain,' she said.

'No, I want to. I've wanted to for a long time. I thought about writing to you.'

The air had cooled. Morning was only a few hours away. The driver was waiting with his white gloves.

'It was nice to see you again,' said Yaping.

'Nice to see you too.'

Mei climbed into the back seat of the car. The leather felt cold.

'Would you like some music, miss?' the driver asked. They were cruising past the villas of the diplomatic quarter. Flags were down. Lights were out, guards off duty.

'Please.' Mei leaned back and closed her eyes.

The sensual sound of a jazz vocal floated from the car stereo. Outside, the dark streets ran silently, leaving behind the darkened lamps. The night was blue. A glow had appeared at the edge of the sky. It beckoned in the distance, beyond her grasp.

25

Mei woke with a headache. She didn't remember drinking much wine. She couldn't have had even half a glass. Yet her head was heavy.

She walked over to the window and opened it. The sound of traffic gushed in as if it were passing through her living room. While she had been asleep, the world five storeys below had burst into life. She stuck a hand outside and felt the warm sunshine. Such was the madness of a Beijing spring, she thought. One day it was wintry and the next day it was the prelude to summer.

Mei was just about to leave when the phone rang. It was Lu.

'Mama is worse. They are transferring her to No. 301 Hospital.'

'What happened? She was doing fine yesterday.'

'I don't know. Neither does Little Auntie. They just told her what they were going to do, no explanation. I'm waiting for the duty doctor to call back, if he ever does.'

'Shouldn't they have consulted us before doing something like this?' Fury rose inside Mei's chest, her voice strained, her breathing grew fast.

'Yes, they should have. But they didn't, okay? It doesn't help for us to argue about procedures!'

'Why are you mad at me?' Mei snapped.

'Well, I'm mad at everyone. Little Auntie is quite useless when it comes to something like this. And where have you been?'

'Oh, I can't believe this. Are you blaming me for not being there?' Mei retorted. 'Why weren't *you* there? You said you would go to the hospital yesterday, so I didn't.'

'Well, I have a lot of responsibilities.'

Mei felt her body tense up and her arms began to tremble. She wanted to slam down the telephone.

But she found it difficult to rebuff Lu. What she said was true. Nothing had prevented Mei from being at her mother's side. She didn't have a career as such. She had no family, no one to protect or please. Yet she had still failed to do the one duty required of a daughter, to care for her mother. She regretted not going to the hospital the previous night; she wished more than anything else that she had. She relaxed her grip on the telephone, suddenly overwhelmed with remorse.

'You're right. There's no point in us fighting. I'll go to 309 – I was just on my way there anyway,' said Mei.

'I will go to 301.'

They hung up. Mei shut the door, locking it a few times, and then flew down the stairs. A little boy was sitting on the steps drawing circles with a piece of chalk. Mei almost knocked him over.

She got into her car. When she tried to turn the key in the ignition her hands were shaking. On the road, people passed by on bicycles laden with shopping. Kids were playing and neighbours chatted in the sunshine. She turned the key again. The engine roared. Seconds later, with rubber burning and dirt flying, she drove off.

At No. 309 Hospital, Mei paid ten yuan for a visiting ticket from the sleepy soldier at the ticket booth. She waved it at the guard and walked inside. She ran up the stairs and into the long dark corridor. The nurse's office was open, but empty.

Standing in the middle of the dark hallway, Mei suddenly noticed the silence. All the doors were shut. There was no one about. No hot water trolleys, no relatives sleeping on the floor. It was as if an evacuation had taken place, or she was standing in an abandoned building listening to the lapse of time.

Her heart tightened – not for herself, but for her mother. The empty, whitewashed walls seemed to be staring at her; in her mind she began to draw crazy patterns on them.

She turned abruptly, walking briskly down the hall, going right and crossing the skyway to the doctor's office. Voices came out of the room, a woman was laughing, some men talking. Mei pushed the door open and saw the long table with a few items on it – a mug, a rumpled newspaper, a pile of roasted sunflower seeds, a smaller pile of empty shells, a pair of shoeless feet with a toe poking out from a black sock.

The TV was on and the doctor, his mouth open, nostrils widening and contracting, was dozing. His glasses had slipped to the side. Mei knocked on the door panel and he opened his eyes. It was the same young doctor with whom Mei had spoken on the first day.

He pulled his feet from the table and sat up, adjusting his glasses. 'Yes?' he asked. He wiped a corner of his mouth with the sleeve of his white coat.

'When was my mother transferred?' Mei asked, looking down at him.

The doctor shifted his glasses. He seemed to have lost his bearings.

'You are . . . Ling Bai's daughter?'

'Yes, one of them.'

He pulled himself further upright in his chair, straightening his back, and looked at his watch. 'Half an hour, or maybe three-quarters of an hour ago.'

'Why? Who made the decision to move her? How bad was she? Why wasn't the family contacted?'

'Hey, hey, slow down, okay?' The doctor stood up, holding his palms out like a barrier to block Mei's stream of interrogation.

'Did we question anything? No. We did what we were told. I can't believe *you* are shouting at *me*!' He tapped his hands on his chest.

'What do you mean?'

'Let's be frank. I was the one who had to write up your mother's medical report and send it up every day. You've got friends in high places, fine. We have no argument with you. After all, we've seen it before. If you've got connections, by all means use them. I would.'

'What are you talking about?' Mei stepped back.

'Didn't you arrange for her to go to No. 301 Hospital? It wasn't our decision to move your mother.'

Mei shook her head. 'No. We didn't know anything about it.'

'Well, that's strange.' The doctor retreated, reaching for his tea mug. He had a sip, frowned, and put it down. It must have gone cold long before.

'This morning, an order came directly from the hospital leadership to move your mother. We figured you must have some important connections.'

'No. It certainly wasn't us. Are you saying that my mother's health has not got worse?'

'She hasn't improved either.'

Now both Mei and the doctor were embarrassed. She smiled awkwardly. He fidgeted with his glasses.

'Well, I'm sorry to have bothered you,' said Mei, hands on her handbag.

'No, not at all.'

They said goodbye politely and turned in opposite directions, puzzled.

26

There had been an accident on the ring-road, a small one, with hardly any damage to either of the cars. But that had not prevented traffic from banking up for miles. When Mei passed the scene three men and two women, the owners of the cars in the crash, were standing by the centre barrier pointing fingers and shouting. Other drivers rolled down their windows as they passed by and joined the argument.

When Mei finally arrived at No. 301 Hospital, she found her sister and Little Auntie outside the intensive care unit.

Little Auntie looked exhausted. The skin of her face had shrunk, making her eyes protrude. She had undoubtedly eaten badly and slept little in the past two days. The pain of watching her sister dying was clearly weighing heavily on her heart.

'Nothing for us to do here. She is isolated, no visitors allowed,' Lu told Mei. 'Have you had breakfast yet? I'm starving.'

Mei thought of the two cups of coffee she had had that morning. 'No,' she said.

'Why don't we go and have a quick bite in the hospital

canteen, and then if they don't need us anymore, we can go home.'

'You two sisters go. I've had my breakfast,' Little Auntie said solemnly. 'I'd rather stick around just in case.'

'I suppose it's not a bad idea for one of us to stay here.' Lu looked first at Mei and then at Little Auntie. 'Are you sure that you don't want us to bring you something from the canteen? Steamed buns, or tea perhaps?'

'I'm okay,' Little Auntie said.

The hospital canteen was on the ground floor of the main building with windows overlooking a small shrub garden. In the garden, a few patients accompanied by family were walking slowly, taking in the sunshine. Behind them was the building housing intensive care.

The canteen had just started to serve lunch. Big pots of meat fried in lard and stacks of hot steamed buns were being delivered. A queue had formed while the kitchen staff busied themselves with pots, steamers and cashboxes. A group of nurses in little white hats came in, holding aluminium bowls and chopsticks. They chatted cheerfully as they stood in line.

Lu laid claim to an empty section of a long table while Mei queued for food. A few white-coats and visitors near them were finishing up their breakfast or snacks. Some of them looked at Lu curiously, probably thinking she looked familiar and wondering where they had seen her before.

Lu wore no make-up, but her lips were tinted. The natural glow of her skin shone through like rosebuds on a clear morning. A beam of sunlight, visible in dancing dust particles, crossed the air behind her.

Mei bought two set-meals, served in the same white plastic containers used for the patients' food trolleys.

'Which one do you want, double-cooked pork with steamed rice or shredded beef with noodles?' Mei had also bought two cans of coconut juice.

'It doesn't matter. I'm so hungry I'd eat anything. Maybe the noodles.'

Lu searched through chopsticks of different lengths and shades in a metal mug on the table.

'These seem to match.' She handed a pair to Mei.

The sisters ate until they were satisfied. Then they relaxed and drank their juice.

'What did the doctor say?' asked Mei.

'Not much. He wanted to do more tests. He's not optimistic but will try his best. He said intensive care is the best place for Mama. They have a designated team of nurses, modern equipment and a doctor on duty around the clock. Should Mama need emergency resuscitation, they can do it without moving her. He said intensive care is especially good for weekends, when the rest of the hospital has a minimum level of staffing.'

'Did he mention anything about money?' Mei asked, remembering her encounter with the young doctor at No. 309 three days ago.

'No. Little Auntie signed some paperwork and then I signed a couple of forms, the usual stuff, as we did at No. 309.'

'Don't you think there's something strange about this? First, No. 309 Hospital wanted us to pay for her medical expenses. Now she is transferred to the best military hospital in China and no one has asked us to pay for anything.'

The juice was cool and soothing to the last drop. The canteen buzzed with noises of all kinds: serious voices, the sounds of eating, the loudspeaker in the corner calling for doctors and nurses.

Lu shrugged a shoulder. 'Of course I think it's strange. Mama does illustrations for magazines and books. She is hardly famous or rich.'

'Maybe she knows people of high ranks. You know, people who have power.'

Lu didn't answer, choosing to follow her own thoughts. 'Most of Mama's friends are useless artists. They have no connections or money. All they can offer is one of their paintings. Though maybe some will be worth something one day.

'Remember when I graduated from college, I was assigned to Beijing Mental Hospital? Mama tried to help, but she had no strings to pull. Eventually I got myself out. I took every opportunity, tried every angle, begged and paid my dues. I had to spend a whole year in that depressing place. No, our mama does not have the kinds of connections that can do all this for her.'

Mei leaned forward and put her arms on the table. 'I wonder if it has something to do with Song Kaishan? I think there's something very peculiar about him. He appears from nowhere with Uncle Chen, and the next thing we know, Mama is being given the best of care: her rank is no longer a problem, her medical bills are paid for. But why?'

'You're the detective. You work it out.'

The two sisters were silent, lost for ideas.

'What should we do with Little Auntie?' Mei asked at last.

'I'll take her home for tonight and then we'll see,' said Lu.

As she spoke she turned her head around and tossed her long honey-brown hair over her shoulder. A gleam of a smile, barely visible, appeared at the corner of her mouth. Mei understood immediately. Perhaps the key to the mystery had been in front of them all along.

'Little Auntie!' they said simultaneously.

'Come over for dinner this evening,' said Lu, 'and we'll make her talk.'

'What about Lining?'

'Don't worry about him. He's leaving for a business trip this afternoon.'

'He's travelling on a Saturday?'

'Flying to America. Oh, look at the time! I want to see him before he goes to the airport.'

Back at intensive care they found Little Auntie dozing in a chair outside the entrance. Someone had just mopped the floor. The room was cool.

Little Auntie's eyes moved wildly as she woke up. 'I thought you were the doctors.'

'Little Auntie, what do you think about this? You come with me to my apartment. I'll send my assistant to fetch your luggage from the hotel. Mei will come for dinner and we can talk about what to do from here. This way you can also have a rest and call Shanghai.'

'It's for the best,' said Mei.

Little Auntie agreed. She picked up the leather carry bag that was sitting by her chair.

'Let me take that for you,' offered Mei.

'No need. It's not heavy,' Little Auntie said.

The three Wang women walked away. They had been cut off from their mother and sister. The thought of Ling Bai lying alone inside an unknown room weighed heavily on their steps.

27

Back on Renaissance Boulevard and on the ring-road, Mei had the feeling that her life was being tangled up in a web too big to comprehend. She thought about Yaping, his chauffeured car and the luxurious Great Wall Hotel. She thought about the big-bellied Won Ton Queen; she liked the name Coming of Spring. She thought about the child-like face of Lili, her strange giggle. Again, she pictured the white eyes of Zhang Hong, his pink scar and bluish face.

Spring had definitely arrived. Mei could have sworn that on the banks of the City Moat tender green hues had appeared on willows that had been bare the day before.

But there was no colour where her mother was lying, in a bleached white box with white coats and little nurse hats. Only an arm's length away, separated by a brick wall and a thin glass window, but divided by a lifetime, the sweet smell of spring was bouncing on sunbeams like transparent butterflies.

Mei turned off the ring-road. As she went down the flyover,

the swirling city engulfed her like a tidal wave, dispersing her sorrows with its chaotic energy.

Mei stopped by the side of her apartment building and cut the engine. The residence village was quiet at siesta time. Mei got out, inhaling a lungful of spring dust. Her throat was dry. She needed a drink.

She went up the dark stairs and opened the door of her apartment. The window was still ajar. Noise poured in from the ring-road. She found a can of Coke in the fridge. She popped it open and drank it down, at the same time hearing a knock at the door.

It was Yaping. His tall figure was dressed in a white shirt and a pair of chinos. A mass of red roses bloomed in his hands. He looked cool and polished, every bit as attractive as he had looked the previous night.

'I was on my way to the airport and thought I should drop in and try my luck,' he said.

'But this is not on the way to the airport.'

'In that case we'd better hurry. Let me take you somewhere we can talk.'

Mei hesitated.

'Please,' Yaping implored. 'I've come all this way, and these roses cost me a fortune.'

That made her laugh. 'All right.' She took the roses. 'Let me put them in water first.' She went to look for a vase. Yaping leaned against the edge of the door.

'How is your mother?' he asked, crossing his arms.

'She's been transferred to intensive care at No. 301 Hospital. It's the best she could have. We hope this means she'll make a recovery.'

'I'm glad to hear it. Please give her my best the next time you see her.'

Mei nodded, though she was not quite sure how her mother would respond to such a greeting.

Outside the Workers' Stadium, vendors were setting up their booths. Crates of bottled water, cola and fizzy fruit drinks were being unloaded. A fast-talking woman was giving orders to do with laying out plum candies, dried fruits, roasted peanuts and sunflower seeds.

The stadium was yet to open.

Yaping asked Mei to wait for him by the gate and disappeared into the ticket office. A few minutes later, he came out with a man in a suit. They were laughing. The man unlocked a side door.

'Just for twenty minutes,' Yaping told him. He was very polite but he had an air of authority.

'No problem, sir, take as long as you need.' The man nodded. He was a young man with an old man's posture.

'How did you get him to open the door for you?' Mei asked Yaping once they were inside.

'With a thick stack of money,' replied Yaping.

The stadium was flooded in bright sunlight and miles of emptiness.

Yaping smiled. 'Do you remember the football game we watched here? It was the World Cup group qualifier, China versus South Korea. I remember it like yesterday. You screamed and cheered just like everyone else. I don't think I had ever seen you like that before.'

Mei shook her head. 'I don't remember,' she lied.

But she did remember. That day the stadium was packed and loud. There were handkerchiefs waving everywhere. There were drums. It was the first and only time she had been here.

They started to walk along the barrier. A long way down, a few indistinct figures were preparing the pitch for the afternoon game. The white lines were brilliant under the sun, so sharp they hurt the eyes.

'It was a very hot day. Then the rain came. I went to America.' Yaping leaned over the bar into the warm space they shared between them.

'And you stopped writing,' said Mei, staring at Yaping's profile. His mouth looked soft in the light. A strand of hair had fallen gently over his forehead. But there was a lost expression in his eyes.

They sat down on one of the benches.

'I felt I could never be good enough for you,' Yaping said. 'You always made me feel inferior. No matter how I tried to impress you, your bar was always higher.'

'Oh, so it was my fault.'

'No, it was me. I was young and insecure, a boy from the south, a small-town kid. I got hurt easily.' Yaping took a deep breath. His shoulders dropped. 'I met my wife – I should say, ex-wife – on the plane to Chicago. To my surprise, she pursued me. I was flattered; she thought I was worth something. It was a nice change, to be sought after, not to have to prove myself – and, as stupid as it may sound, I liked being needed. You never needed me or anyone. I felt useless around you. And sometimes, you shut off. I couldn't reach you. It was as if you wanted to push me away. Is it so unreasonable for a man to want intimacy, to want to help and protect the woman he loves?'

Mei frowned. 'You'd rather be with someone who is weak?'

'No, that's not what I mean. I am a man, do you understand? I am supposed to be your protector.'

'I can look after myself,' Mei retorted.

Yaping shook his head and sighed. 'I knew you wouldn't understand. But it doesn't matter. As I was saying, I was far away from home and alone in a new world. I needed warmth and confidence. Then came the student democracy movement. When we saw TV reports of the student hunger strike in Tiananmen Square, the Chinese students in Chicago got organised. We raised money and demonstrated outside the Chinese Embassy. There is something about a tumultuous time that bonds people together. We fell in love.'

'What happened then? Why did you divorce?'

'Well, people change.' Yaping gazed into the empty stadium as if his thoughts had been carried far away.

'Have I changed?' asked Mei, tilting her head to one side. As she did so, she felt something had touched her hair. It was the sleeve of Yaping's shirt.

'I don't know yet. But I know I have.'

From nowhere a little sparrow had come, pattering his tiny brown feet joyously across the benches.

'I'm not sure whether we actually change,' said Mei. 'When we say that we've changed, perhaps we mean that our understanding of the world has changed. Remember when we were young, we used to speak of forever? We pledged to love each other forever and to remember each other forever. I'm not saying that we didn't mean it. We were sincere about what we said. Only we had no idea what forever was. It was just a word that we used, like rain or wind, something that existed, something convenient.'

Yaping turned to look intently at Mei as she spoke.

'Now I have seen forever and, believe me, it has no beauty or glamour. Forever is what true sorrow is made of. Watching my mother in the hospital, I saw forever coming. It came so close that

I could have touched it. When someone dies, they disappear. Death is forever, irreversible and final. Once it happens, nothing can change it. Forever is the end of all possibilities, where no wrongs can be righted and no regrets can be pardoned.

'When I watched life slipping away from my mother, something departed from me too. You know about my family. My mother raised me and my sister on her own. We struggled a lot. For years we lived in temporary housing, often with only little to eat and sometimes no money to buy new clothes for school.'

She looked out at the deserted, sunlit stadium. For a few seconds her thoughts drifted.

'Thinking about the past makes me feel very sad, especially since, as you probably remember, I have not had the best relationship with my mother. Now that she is seriously ill, I realise that there is so much I don't know about her and so much I want to say to her.

'Every time I see a thread of new sunshine, a leaf's new green or a flower budding, I think of my mother and how she may not be here to see them again. And I think of the next day, the next year, when all these things will happen again, and life will renew itself as if it had no memory. The world will continue, I will continue, but she will not.'

Mei fell silent. She had forgotten what point she was making. Whatever it was, it no longer mattered. At that moment she came to understand why she had been searching for her mother everywhere she went. She had conjured up her presence in street-centre parks and in morning markets, and as she walked through narrow, winding alleys, turning corners, she saw her mother and the loneliness in her glances.

In the distance, a siren screamed then faded and vanished like a memory.

'You really love her, don't you?' said Yaping. Mei's voice had come to him like wind over grassland, like a lost love on its way home, softer and clearer than in his dreams.

'I guess so. I don't know. Maybe this is what people call love. But I don't think of it in that way. To me, this is just the way things are, the way they are supposed to be. I don't have a choice. My mother is like a lighthouse. No matter how far I try to get away from her, I seem to be always coming back.'

'Are you going to be okay?'

'You mean if my mother dies? I don't know. I'm a survivor – at least, I like to think I am. I have dealt with tough times before, when you got married and when I resigned from the Ministry. But this time it's different.'

Mei saw the slightest frown gathering between Yaping's eyes.

'I suppose I should explain why I left my old job.'

He nodded. 'I would like to understand.'

'When I was working at the Ministry for Public Security, my title was Personal Assistant to the Head of Public Relations. It was in many ways an interesting and luxurious job. I had the glamour but not the sweat of working on the ground. Mostly I relayed orders and requests to local offices and looked after major events and showcases. I liaised with foreign visitors and accompanied my boss to meetings at the Ministry.

'My boss wasn't brilliant but he wasn't bad to work with either. Our relationship was cordial. We lived inside the same compound. I had many meals at his home and was friendly with his family. One thing you need to understand is that for a bureaucrat like him he had reached a critical age. If he could rise up further, he would be hailed as young for a ministerial position. But if he failed to break through, he would quickly be considered old and he would have to make way for the younger generation.

'I am explaining this to you so you'll understand why it was such a big deal when it happened. As I said, as his PA I often accompanied my boss to ministerial-level meetings. Naturally I met many important people, including ministers.

'To cut a long story short, one of the ministers had, according to my boss, taken a fancy to me and wanted me to be his mistress. Oh, yes, this is quite common now, especially when the man has money or power. I won't tell you his name. You have been away from China for too long; you won't know him. But it doesn't matter. I said no. And when my boss couldn't convince me to change my mind, he told me that he would make me suffer until I agreed. You see, I had become the bridge that could take him to the top of the Ministry. So I was banished to the field and harassed constantly. The rumour mill was working overtime. You can't imagine the ugly lies that were told about me. I still feel sick thinking about it. I had no more friends. People avoided me like I was a disease.

'It was like black water flooding in to fill an underground cave. Every space, every opening of my life was being taken over. I couldn't escape. So I resigned. It didn't stop the lies, of course. They reached far and wide. But they could no longer do me harm. I cut people out of my life. I cut my life out of other people's. Sometimes I think I am rather good at this and prefer it that way. I think I have a hard shell. In some ways, I've probably had it since I was five years old.

'But what I have to face now with Mama is even worse. Where can I go? How can I escape the death of someone I love?'

'Maybe you can't.' Yaping leaned close to her. Mei could feel the warmth of his body and see the muscles under his shirt. Suddenly she wished he would touch her, although she felt that, if he did, she would break into a million pieces.

'Sometimes you can't protect yourself from pain.' His words rolled down her neck like loose pearls. 'Avoiding it will only make you hurt more. No, I'm not trying to give you advice. I can't possibly understand how you feel. All I'm saying is that sometimes being part of something painful is in fact what helps us to survive. It helps us to go on with our lives.'

'You are probably right,' Mei replied. 'But I just can't think about survival, not now. It's inconsistent, I know. I think too much about death and forever. But the more I think about them, the more I feel that I can't live without her. She is the closest thing I have to affection, sad as it may be. The world is a cold place, for me at least. It would be so much colder without her.'

They were silent. Sunlight spread across the vast space in front of them in waves like music, some notes higher than others, in a serene harmony.

Mei had told Yaping things that she had never told anyone else. She couldn't understand why she did it. 'I'm sorry that I talked so much about myself. You've got a plane to catch,' she said, pulling herself together.

'No, *I* am sorry. I wish that we could stay like this and talk for a long time. Over the years I have imagined many conversations like this. In a way they have all been part of a very long conversation that is still going on. I am terribly sorry about your mother.'

They stood up. The sun was warm, caressing their backs like lovers' hands. A sad silence began to divide the minutes into halves and then halves again until there was no time left.

'I may come back to Beijing to work,' Yaping said. 'My firm wants to grow our Asian practice and open an office here.'

When they reached the car, Yaping took his luggage from the boot. 'I will take a taxi to the airport. Mr Lui here can drive you anywhere you'd like. He's been paid for the day.'

The driver nodded politely from behind the steering wheel, his gloves spotlessly white.

'Goodbye, Mei.' Yaping gave her his hand.

'Goodbye.' She gave him hers.

Besieged by white sunlight, they stood holding hands, remembering a promise that had slipped away once before, a time long ago.

28

The porter in Lu's building had a moon face, a warm smile and, it seemed, an amazing memory. He greeted Mei by name as soon as she stepped into the lobby.

'Miss Wang, long time no see. What's it been? Half a year at least?' The porter nodded, twisting a pencil in his hands. His blue uniform had been neatly pressed. He had heard about Ling Bai's stroke and offered his condolences.

'What a pity.' He shook his head. 'They had it bad – the older generation, I mean. First it was the Great Leap Forward, nothing to eat; then the Cultural Revolution, struggling and beating every day. Finally life gets better, sons and daughters are prospering, and now this. Pity, I say. People like your mother suffered all their lives, no wonder they now have rotten health.'

He sighed, twitching his pencil. 'Your sister has gone out, but she said if you are here, you should go straight up.' He bowed slightly.

Mei followed him to the lift.

'Lu is such a devoted daughter. It's heartbreaking to see her so worried,' said the porter.

Behind them the giant glass door opened and in came a young man of about twenty with a bottle-bleached head and a slightly younger girl with a pair of oversized sunglasses and baby-doll pink hair. The man was carrying a golf bag as big as himself. A set of clubs was neatly hidden beneath fluffy yellow duck club warmers. There were also two pink club warmers with pom-poms, presumably hers.

The porter quickly called the lift for them, smiling at the newcomers. The girl bowed while the guy returned a courteous hello. No one spoke again. The penthouse lift appeared quickly. 'Thank you,' Mei said as she stepped inside.

She wanted to say more, to return the porter's kindness. But before she could speak, the door had shut. She was moving up.

With a ding, the lift arrived. Mei stepped out. A spotless beige carpet stretched into a white hallway. Lights like crystal balls were spaced along the walls. There was no sound, only the pale harmony of silent perfection.

Mei rang the doorbell and waited.

'Oh, Mei, you're here!' exclaimed the housekeeper, opening the door as wide as her smile.

A light aroma of ginger and clove greeted Mei's senses. The sunlight had grown deeper and warmer hues, and pasted itself on the floor-to-ceiling windows.

'Your aunt's sleeping,' said the housekeeper.

Mei nodded and handed over her bag and jacket. 'How are you, Auntie Zhang?' Mei leaned her head to the side so that her words could follow the housekeeper as she started to walk away. 'You look like you've lost weight.'

'Really?' Auntie Zhang turned back. She smoothed down her floral shirt. 'You think so?' She was pleased.

Auntie Zhang was in her fifties. She had long limbs, with large hands and feet. She had worked for Lu for many years, first doing cleaning and cooking and then, after Lu had married, as the housekeeper, overseeing the cleaners and the cook.

She looked at Mei with a gentleness that helped to soften her rustic features. 'I know you are worried about your mother.' She pulled a pair of white flannel slippers from the shoe cabinet. 'But listen to your Auntie, you've got to look after yourself. I say the same to Lu. You can't let it crush you. Or your mother will not have you to depend on.'

Mei put on the slippers. They were as new as virgin snow.

Auntie Zhang pointed her chin towards the window. 'Go sit down. I'll bring you some tea.'

Mei took two steps down to the living room. Long antique side tables of red lacquer lined the walls. Objects glittered from all sides: a gold Buddha, a pair of antique wine goblets, two Tang Dynasty tri-colour porcelain horses, a Chinese wedding box painted in real gold (so Lu said), a Bang & Olufsen stereo system, awards, trophies and pictures in shining frames. There were two pots of white orchids on hourglass flower stands, each with twenty blossoms. The ceiling was so high that it made her feel dizzy.

Mei sat on the sofa beneath a Warhol-style portrait of Lu. It was strange to see Lu on the wall instead of Mao Zhedong or Marilyn Monroe.

Mei picked up a lavish book on the Yangtze River from the coffee table and flipped through the pages. On one page she saw a lone junk with her giant yellow sail, poised on the verge of a dark expanse of water; Mei was struck by its lonely magnificence. A few pages further on there were pictures of the famous grottos and 'to heaven' paths. These paths were chiselled from the faces of vertical cliffs; for centuries, armies had loyally marched along them. Locals believe, the text explained, that at night they can still hear the ghosts of dead soldiers toiling up the cliffs.

All of these would soon be under water and gone forever when the Three Gorges Dam was completed. Mei thought that she ought to go and see the river for herself before it was too late.

'Here's your tea.' Auntie Zhang came in with a tray on which sat a cast-iron teapot and delicate teacups rimmed with gold.

'Where is Lu?' asked Mei.

'She went to the beauty spa, but she should be back soon.'

Auntie Zhang poured the first cup, green as the valley. 'Drink slowly,' she said. 'If you don't need me, I must go and help the cook.'

The two women smiled at each other. Then Auntie Zhang walked away, swinging her long arms.

Mei took her tea to the window. Pink twilight covered the rooftops of Beijing. This part of the city had always felt alien to her, with its walled villas, foreign embassies and the showcase architecture along the Boulevard of Eternal Peace. She hadn't set foot in the area until her senior year in university. A Japanese exchange student had taken her shopping to the Friendship Store, a shop dedicated to foreigners, two blocks south of here on Inner Jianguo Gate Boulevard.

It was the first time that Mei had been inside the Friendship Store. She couldn't believe her eyes. The marbled halls were filled with things she had never seen before – gold, pearls, Spanish shoes, American sportswear, cosmetics and perfumes, all of which were extraordinarily expensive. Her companion had brought coupons to the value of fifty thousand Japanese yen. Mei could hardly remember her date now except that he always wore a long black coat and that he was a good cook. He had taught her to make sushi.

'Mei.' A soft voice spoke behind her.

Mei turned and saw Little Auntie. She was wearing a newly pressed blue shirt. Her black hair glowed from being washed and conditioned.

'How did you sleep?'

'Soundly, like I've not slept for days.' Little Auntie sounded cheerful.

'There is tea, but it's getting cold. Perhaps Auntie Zhang could make you another pot?'

'No. I've had plenty of tea.'

They sat down on the sofa. Mei inquired about Little Auntie's family and whether there had been news when she phoned them that afternoon. They exchanged news of other relatives. Somewhere in the background they heard the soft clink of china and glasses. Auntie Zhang must be laying the table for dinner in the dining room.

'Is dinner ready?' Lu's singing voice startled them. They turned around and saw her standing at the top of the steps in a pink dress. It was as if a piece of the burning sky had broken away and drifted inside with her. Her long hair shone and glittered with reflected light. 'I'm starving!' Kicking off her high-heeled shoes, she waved at her sister and aunt.

Auntie Zhang brought Lu her lambskin slippers. 'It's ready. It's ready.' She nodded.

'Good. Mei! Little Auntie!' Lu gestured to them. 'Come, let's eat now.' She apologised for being late. 'My manicurist was sick today, so I had to take someone else. She didn't understand what I wanted done. Oh, what a headache!'

She took Little Auntie by the arm and said sweetly,

'Tomorrow, why don't you go to the spa with my membership card? Get yourself a facial, a haircut or anything you'd like.'

They entered the dining room. A long rosewood table had been covered with a tablecloth and laid with sparkling glass and ivory-tipped chopsticks. The walls were white and decorated with abstract oil paintings. A chandelier, so large that it looked more suited to a ballroom, hung from the ceiling.

Auntie Zhang and a stout woman were bringing in dishes served on Ming-blue plates.

'You've got to try this new treatment called seaweed wrapping,' Lu said to Mei after they took their seats at the table. 'It's fantastic, guaranteed to get rid of negative energy and cellulite.'

'Really?' Mei said politely.

'I know you think beauty spas are contrived. But, my dear sister, we can all use some help from time to time, especially once we are of a certain age.' Lu gave her sister a wink and smiled.

Auntie Zhang came around with snow-white rice.

Lu said to her guests, 'I was reading *Beijing Late Edition* at my spa. It said that the government has ordered all small stock-trading outposts to close. It looks like they are finally going to crack down on stir-frying stock.'

Little Auntie nodded, looking at first at Lu and then Mei. 'These days in Shanghai everyone is stir-frying stock. As soon as the trading outposts open in the morning, all the grandmothers line up to buy and sell.'

'They trade stocks like betting on horses at the racetrack,' Lu said. 'Most of the small investors are ignorant. Take these grandmothers, for example; they are barely educated. What do they know about the stock market? After all, the stock market is not the morning market.

'Well, you find the same problem in business,' she went on.

'There are so many companies these days, building hotels, apartments, offices and sometimes roads. Some can be quite crooked and would do anything for money. The government ought to be careful as to whom these projects are given. No, it's not monopoly or elitism. It's like what the Party Central has said – capitalism with a socialist orientation. If the government can regulate and let good businessmen run the economy, China can only do better. Look at Singapore. Highly educated people are more valued because, well, let's face it, they *are* better.

'When Lining and I are abroad, people always say, "You are so cosmopolitan." They see us as representatives of modern China.'

Little Auntie nodded. 'People like you and Lining are smart.'

'But we also work very hard,' said Lu. 'Elitism is wrong if those who are special don't fulfil their responsibilities. We are the role models, we mustn't forget that.'

After dinner, they were served jasmine tea in the living room. On the coffee table Auntie Zhang laid out roasted sunflower seeds, dried lychees and saltwater peanuts in crystal bowls.

'Thank you for a wonderful dinner,' Little Auntie said. She sat back carefully so as not to spill tea on Lu's white goose-down sofa.

'Our cook is really very good, isn't she? I'll tell her that you enjoyed her cooking. It's such a shame that Lining and I don't dine at home more often.' Lu spoke softly, sipping tea from her gold-rimmed teacup.

'Mei, what do you think of my new floor?' Lu smiled, tilting her head a little. 'I've just had it done. Everyone is doing marble floors now.' She pointed at the floor with her red manicured fingers. 'These stones are imported from Italy.'

'Very nice,' said Little Auntie, nodding. She was noisily cracking roasted sunflower seeds between her teeth.

'At first I didn't want to bother with it; after all, we'll be moving soon. But then, you know me, I do hate to compromise.'

'You're moving? But you haven't lived here for two years.' There was always something happening with Lu: another jade or ruby, a newer car, a better looking assistant, more desirable friends. Mei could hardly keep up.

'We have bought an apartment in the new development called Jianguo Tower on Jianguo Gate Boulevard. In fact, we signed the contract yesterday. Do you know the one, Mei? You must have seen it. It's huge.'

'But why move for a few blocks? This apartment is lovely.'

'Oh, my dear sister. Jiangou Gate Boulevard is Beijing's Park Avenue. Jianguo Tower is going to be the only apartment building allowed inside Jianguo Gate. People are already talking about it. You will see, Jianguo Tower will be the ultimate address in Beijing.'

'The apartments must be very expensive,' said Little Auntie enviously.

'They are, and you have to be approved by the management. They only want the most respected citizens.' Lu was becoming more animated. Her face glowed with self-satisfaction.

Mei looked at her, aghast. 'Was that why you didn't go see Mama yesterday? Because you were buying a new apartment?'

'It was important. We had been waiting for months to get approval.'

'More important than looking after your own mother?' Mei snapped.

'Don't you criticise me. You were not there yourself,' Lu retorted.

'You're so selfish. All you ever care about is yourself. "Oh dear, I can't go see my mother, who is dying, because I've got to go buy a bigger and better apartment."'

'*I* am selfish?' Lu stood up, her almond eyes burning with anger. 'What have you done for Mama? I've brought Little Auntie from Shanghai and paid for all her expenses. I would have paid for Mama's medical bills too. I could very well save her life. What can you do? Nothing. Because you have nothing. You are a big failure. In fact, all you've ever done is give Mama grief. It is probably because of you that she is in the hospital!'

Mei stood up. 'How dare you? I love Mama. I'd do anything for her. You are a success because you've used everyone you've ever met!'

'Girls, girls!' Little Auntie stood up, waving her arms like a madwoman. 'Stop this nonsense at once!' she shouted. 'You're breaking your mother's heart.' Tears suddenly rolled down her cheeks. 'Have you any idea what your mother has gone through? This is not right, not after what she's done for you.'

Mei and Lu each took an arm and helped Little Auntie to sit down on the sofa. Lu quickly brought a packet of tissues. Little Auntie cried, sometimes groaning painfully, pressing her chest, sometimes quietly weeping. The sisters watched the tears pour down her cheeks as if without end. They were shocked that their aunt, who they'd always known as the happy little sister of their mother, could harbour so much grief inside her tiny body. Her shoulders shook, her eyes were red and full of sorrow.

'Tell us about it,' said Mei. She glanced at her sister. She hadn't forgiven her, but now they had to put aside their argument and talk to Little Auntie.

'We want to know,' said Lu.

Little Auntie shook her head. 'I promised your mother . . .'

'Little Auntie . . .' There was authority in Lu's sweet voice. 'I know that Mama would not have wanted to keep any secrets from me if she knew that she was going to die.'

Mei poured a cup of tea for Little Auntie. The fragrance of jasmine filled the air. 'Little Auntie, please tell us. We've already discovered a lot. We know that Mama and Uncle Chen used to work together. When was that? What did Mama do?'

Slowly Little Auntie stopped sobbing. She wiped her face with a clean tissue and took the teacup.

'I'll have to start from the beginning,' she said quietly, staring at the sunflower seeds inside the crystal bowl as if she were talking only to them.

Her nieces nodded. The pressure in the room had become so intense it felt as though another word or a simple movement might make their confrontation collapse.

Slowly, softly, Little Auntie began. 'Your mother was chosen by the Ministry for State Security before she even graduated from university. She was fluent in Russian, a driven and brilliant student, and also the class Communist Party representative. Yes, she went into the secret service. It was a very prestigious job, as you can imagine.

'Naturally there was a lot of secrecy. She could never tell me exactly what she did or even where she was sometimes. But I knew she was happy. She made new friends and reconnected with old friends like Uncle Chen, who also joined the Ministry. And she met your father, a young writer on the rise, dashing and intelligent. Your mother fell deeply in love.

'Then came the Cultural Revolution. Suddenly the establishment, what we used to call the Old Guards, became the enemy of the state. I joined the Red Guard, as did millions of other fourteen-year-olds. We travelled around the country, rebelling against the old. Before long the entire country was being turned upside down. Then your father was exposed and sent to a hard-labour camp for his anti-Mao views. Your mother went with him, taking both of you.

'When she finally came back to Beijing, she had been sick for a while and had lost a lot of weight. I don't know how your mother saved you from the hard-labour camp; she never talked about it. But I know that she must have gone through hell for that. You didn't just "get out" of a hard-labour camp.

'She had changed. Your mother was beautiful in her younger years. But when I saw her again after the labour camp, she looked old and her beauty was gone. She was sad and tried very hard to escape from the misery that seemed to consume her. She had lost her home, her husband and her job. She had no hope, except for the two of you.

'You probably don't remember how hard it was when you were growing up. You were always being moved around to wherever there was a vacant room, and you never had enough to eat. Your mother struggled a lot, until eventually she was allocated the job at the magazine.'

'What happened to Mama's job at the Ministry for State Security?' asked Mei.

'She lost it. Because she was married to your father and had gone to the labour camp with him, she was no longer a red revolutionary. She couldn't work for the Ministry for State Security anymore.'

'But why is the Ministry looking after her now?' Lu asked, her almond eyes shining.

'I don't know whether it is the Ministry. She hasn't had anything to do with them for twenty-five years.' Little Auntie was reluctant to say more.

'But who else could have such power?' Lu frowned.

Little Auntie shook her head. 'Whoever it is, I wish he had come to her earlier. Then she wouldn't have suffered so much. My poor Big Sister. She was lonely and losing her health. It shouldn't have been like this. She was supposed to have everything: beauty, talent, passion and a bright future. But she had to marry your ba.'

'Do you know what happened to him?' For twenty years, Mei had been waiting for someone to tell her the answer. 'How did he die?'

'I don't know, and frankly I don't think you should ask about him. Not now. Why do you always care so much about your ba? This is what saddens your mama always. Your ba is dead and he ruined your lives. Your mother is the one who has suffered, loved and raised you. I hope you understand the hardship she had to go through. She has climbed a mountain of knives and dived into a sea of fire for the two of you. You are here today because she chose you. She chose to love you.'

As Little Auntie uttered these words, she began to cry again. Her sister had loved her too. And now she who had been so tough and generous was dying.

29

Mei walked briskly along the walls of the Ancient Praying Hall. The morning was still cool from the night's touch. The old and sick had come to the park to exercise, swinging their arms. A group of middle-aged women practised with swords in a square. By a small lake, a young man was standing at the edge of a pavilion singing Beijing Opera.

The tranquil sunlight, the sparrows dashing between the trees and the vague bells from the Lama Temple all seemed to belong to a fairytale.

'Morning!'

'Out walking birds?'

Two men greeted each other. They tossed their birdcages up and down. They wore white mandarin-collared shirts and dark trousers.

It was in the square beyond the trees, amongst the birdmen and their birdcages hanging from the branches, with the singing of blue jays and yellow canaries filling the air, that Mei found Uncle Chen.

Uncle Chen was doing *Tai Chi* with a group of about fifty people. From a distance, they looked like a crowd having a slow race. Everyone squatted. With his back turned, their teacher moved, oblivious to his pupils. The disciples copied his movements precisely and quietly.

Uncle Chen's beige tracksuit squeezed his stomach like a friend, leaving him little space to breathe. When he saw Mei, he stopped his silk weaving, bowed apologetically and zigzagged out of the group.

'Auntie Chen said I could find you here,' said Mei.

'It's your auntie's idea that I do *Tai Chi*. To lose weight, she says. Honestly I'd rather sleep in on a Sunday.' Uncle Chen wiped the sweat from his forehead with the sleeve of his tracksuit.

'Is there somewhere we can talk?'

'Sure, have you had breakfast?'

Mei shook her head.

They walked towards the east gate, against the tide of swinging arms. Some of them threw a word of hello or a knowing nod at Uncle Chen, who reciprocated elaborately. There was pride in his eyes. Walking next to Mei, he carried himself not wide, but tall.

Mobile vendors had set up their stoves on Beautiful Food Street. Squares of bean curd and spicy beef sizzled on iron frying plates. Smoke from coal-burning furnaces hung everywhere. Neighbours greeted each other warmly and customers and vendors hollered.

'Does Didi still wet his bed?'

'Thank goodness he's only my grandson.'

Freshly fried red chilli and Sichuan peppercorns sizzled, triggering a cannonade of coughs.

'Boss, go easy on the chilli, would you?' A man fanned the smoke with his hand.

'No spicy, no taste,' shouted the black-eyed man behind the steam.

'We'll go to the teahouse.' Uncle Chen tugged on Mei's arm. 'Your auntie won't let me eat in the street. She thinks those places aren't clean.'

The teahouse had a sagging front and its paint was chipped. They had to shove at the door, which appeared to be jammed. Inside, the room was damp and smoky.

'This one is state-owned. The food is expensive, but it's clean,' said Uncle Chen.

They found a table in the corner. Uncle Chen went to the counter. Five minutes later he came back with two bowls of salt-egg porridge, two steamers of Little Dragon Buns and a small plate of pickles.

Uncle Chen sat down across the table. He pushed a steamer towards Mei and told her to eat. 'Young people like you need to eat to grow strong.'

He spluttered: the porridge was hot.

'Have you found the jade?' Uncle Chen stared at Mei anxiously.

'Actually, I'm not here about the jade.'

'Oh, I thought . . .' Uncle Chen bit into a Little Dragon Bun. A streak of oil trickled from the corner of his mouth. He quickly wiped it off with his hand. 'What is it that you want to talk to me about?' he asked.

Mei poked at the salted eggs with her chopstick, drowning them in porridge. She had no appetite. She watched Uncle Chen devouring the Dragon Buns.

'Who is looking after my mother? Is it the secret service?' she asked.

A slice of pickled radish stuck in his throat and Uncle Chen coughed. 'What made you think that?'

Mei frowned. 'Uncle Chen, I know. My Little Auntie told us. You are one of them.' She pushed over her steamer of Dragon Buns. 'You knew, didn't you? That was why you were not a bit surprised when I told you that my mother had been transferred.'

Uncle Chen buried his face in the porridge bowl. A long silence dropped like a feather.

'Song said he would take care of it,' Uncle Chen said at last, almost inaudibly.

'Who is he?'

Uncle Chen laid his chopsticks on top of the porridge bowl and wiped his face with his pink hands. 'That's an easy question with a hard answer.' He leaned forward. 'You'll never see his picture or even his name mentioned in the newspapers. You look at Song and you think he is a clean middle bureaucrat from some faceless work unit. No. This is a man who could determine life and death if he wanted to.'

Two tables away, people were leaving, scraping chairs on the floor and chatting loudly. Uncle Chen waited until they went out, then continued. 'I followed your mother to Beijing when we went to university. We stayed good friends, but during those years she seemed to have moved ahead. Women mature much faster at that age. By the time she joined the Ministry for State Security, we had drifted apart. Perhaps that was why I fought so hard for the quota to the same ministry. As far as I can remember, that was the only time in my life that I competed for something so determinedly. I believed if I went to the same ministry, I could rekindle the kind of close relationship we had in Shanghai and perhaps one day she'd see me as more than a friend.'

Uncle Chen looked away, his voice becoming irritable.

'But of course the Ministry was huge. Your mother and I did not exactly work together, if that's the word for it. In fact, she worked and lived inside the main West Garden compound while I worked first at a specialised unit near the Purple Bamboo Garden and then at Xinhua News Agency.

'Yet our friendship was renewed because we belonged to the same ministry and did similar kinds of work. We sometimes spent Sundays together. Back then we had a six-day week and Sunday was the only day off. Your mother was popular and had many friends. Soon we all got to know each other. That's how I met Song, who was her group leader at the time.

'Song was two years older than your mother. He was tall, handsome and a star. I didn't like him. Maybe I felt threatened by him – but, then, I felt threatened by a lot of people. There was always something about him that unsettled me. I always had the feeling that I was being watched. Very strange, I know, but that was how I felt. It was as if he had a third eye.

'Three years on, the Cultural Revolution began, and things got much darker. Secret files were being opened and more were being created. People were being denounced for one thing or another, especially if they had said or written anything that could be called anti-revolutionary. Soon people started to die in large numbers, in horrifying ways. I actually knew someone who was beaten to death for wearing foreign-branded cashmere sweaters. The insanity of it all!

'The Cultural Revolution was a shock to your mother. When we were in Luoyang, she was quite taken aback by what was happening on the ground.'

'I thought you said that you went there alone?'

'I didn't want to drag your mother into it, but now you know.

The Red Guard had sandbagged themselves on the roof of the library with machine guns and had dug tunnels under their positions for supply lines. There were so many deaths. People were so young and so full of devotion to Chairman Mao and the Party. Your mother couldn't bear to see those white faces and bloody bodies. She couldn't stand the screams or the sound of bullets roaring. She had just had you. You were so beautiful, a life that had just begun.

'Before long we were all caught like little insects in the ever-tightening web of revolution, being denounced, denouncing others, being sent to labour camps. I lost touch with your mother for a while and thus had no contact with Song. Some years later, I started to hear his name. While we suffered, he had risen to the top of the Ministry.

'Towards the end of the Cultural Revolution, Song was overthrown. Well, the political current at the time was so difficult to navigate, things flip-flapped all the time – one day Deng Xiaoping was a hero; the next day, public enemy number one. So it was not inconceivable that Song could have made miscalculations. When he lost out, his son was sent to the mountains of Dongbei and I heard that he almost died there.

'Then there was the death of his wife. It was kind of mysterious. No one seemed to know the details. For all I know, it could have been Song himself who sent his wife to her death. There was something very cold about him underneath that charming exterior. With some people you just know that they could one day strike with the utmost cruelty.

'His loss of power and his family's suffering made him a victim of the Cultural Revolution, which gave him the credentials to rise again after Chairman Mao died.'

Uncle Chen sighed. 'So there you go. When we started, Song

was just a group leader. Now he is the Deputy Head of the Ministry for State Security, with a big apartment, a chauffeured car and plenty of power.'

'But why does he want to help my mother?'

'My dislike for Song aside, he seems to have behaved well when it comes to your mother. For a while we thought the two of them would get married.

'When your parents met, your father was a promising young writer, a poet of a certain reputation. He was also an idealist, the opposite of people like us, whose job was spying on others. Perhaps even then your mother had unconsciously harboured doubts about her duties and the world she represented. I suppose that was why your father held such allure for her.'

Uncle Chen sighed again, as if life had been one long sigh. 'Your mother was a beautiful woman, talented and full of life. We all loved her. Unfortunately, she loved your father.'

A chubby girl in a dirty apron had stomped over to scoop up empty dishes onto the plastic tray she carried under her arm, banging the bowls and plates carelessly as she went. The sheen of her face carried the air of the back kitchen, heavy with lard and the smell of wind-dried sausages. Mei watched her mopping the tables. Her movements were slack, her whole being was sluggish.

'Should we have some tea?' Mei asked Uncle Chen. Without waiting for an answer, she stood up and moved to the counter, feeling light-headed.

A woman the size of a small elephant slapped a towel on the board. 'Got you!' she exclaimed, flicking away a dead fly with her middle finger. 'What do you want?' she asked Mei unsmilingly. She wiped her hands on the towel.

'A pot of Oolong tea, two cups.' Mei took out her wallet.

The woman marched over to the counter behind her,

snatched a few loose tea-leaves from a tin and dumped them into a brown teapot. She lifted a giant aluminium kettle from the stove and poured hot water into the pot.

'Four yuan.' She slammed the lid back on the teapot and pushed two teacups towards Mei.

Mei handed over the money before the woman could spit at her. As she walked away with the tea she saw Uncle Chen tucking in to the last Dragon Buns. Now she took in his physical form in all its details – the bulging waist, the head that looked like an upside-down egg and his back hunched over the table. *He* was in love with *Mama*? Her stomach contracted. Then she thought of Song, his leanness and elegant stride. There was a controlled charisma in that man.

Holding the tea in her hands, Mei took a long breath and forced a smile. 'Oolong tea?'

She sat down and poured out the tea. Their hands reached for the teacups at the same time. 'Sorry,' they both said, embarrassed.

'Do you know what happened in the labour camp? How did she get us out? And why not my father too?' Mei held her cup next to her heart.

Uncle Chen shook his head. 'I don't know. She never told me. She never wanted to talk about that period of her life.'

He gazed at Mei with all the misery of life in his eyes. 'I'm sorry, Mei. If you don't want to go on with the jade, I'll understand.'

'I'll go on, and I will find it,' Mei snapped.

Her voice faded. They were both silent now. The waitresses had disappeared. The teahouse was empty. A musky aftertaste seemed to settle from nowhere.

'Do you know what the eye of jade is?' Mei asked.

Yesterday, she had called Pu Yan with the same question. But he didn't have the answer. He told Mei that he would ask some of his colleagues and would call her if he learned anything.

Uncle Chen was also puzzled.

'No. I'm afraid not.' He pressed his lips together and shook his head. 'Why?'

'Maybe it's nothing,' Mei said. 'I've got to go, and let you go home to Auntie. She'll think I've kidnapped you.'

Mei rose, quietly pushing back the chair. Uncle Chen looked up. Hidden gloom wavered behind his shallow eyes.

'I'll be in touch,' Mei said.

The door jammed again, so she left it ajar. Outside, the sun had exploded into a thousand pieces of white light.

30

'Boss isn't here,' said the manager at Big Papa Wu's. He was tall, with a nose like a crow's beak. A yard of black silk was draped over his shoulders.

'Are you sure?' Mei's lips curled up. 'Tell him that I've come from the Hotel Splendour.'

He studied her vaguely, his nose twitching. A cloud of suspicion hovered behind his eyes. Eventually he nodded and went back to moving receipts. Behind them, shoppers were murmuring, people were coming and going.

A receipt was brought over and he stamped the store seal on it in red ink. Then he turned and walked away. A door opened and shut noiselessly. The black crow was gone.

The window was open to bright sunshine. Big Papa Wu sat with his back to it, watching Mei from behind a large rectangular table. It looked like an old altar table once placed before a family shrine. It had carved legs and no drawers. There wasn't much on it: an ink pen, a notepad, a telephone, a small porcelain figurine of two People's Liberation Army soldiers – one male and one female – in a ballet pose, a lamp with a silk shade, a packet of cigarettes, a silver lighter and a glass ashtray.

Big Papa Wu spread his fists on the table. His muscles bulged under a polo shirt. He fixed his eyes on Mei.

'What is it you want?'

Mei sat before him in a square-backed rosewood chair.

'Did you kill Zhang Hong? You were in such a hurry to get out of there you almost knocked me over.'

Big Papa Wu's fists slid off the table. He fixed Mei with a long blank gaze. 'He killed himself.'

'Why would he do that? The guy's never had it so good – money, a woman, a new life.'

Big Papa Wu grunted throatily. 'Money? The bastard should have left Beijing while he still had it.'

He reached for the cigarettes, hesitated, tapping his fingers on the packet. He knew that he'd said too much.

'What's your story?' He glared at her.

'Let's see, Zhang Hong gambled away all his money and was in debt. He came to ask you for help, but you refused. Perhaps he threatened to expose you and your smuggling. You shut him up.'

Big Papa Wu jerked his head sideways and spat. 'Bullshit.'

He grabbed the Marlboro pack, tore out a cigarette with his teeth, and seized the silver lighter. 'Let me tell you something. I may be a brute, but I don't kill.' He lit the cigarette. 'Six years of street gangs, eight years of "up mountain, down countryside", you can trust me when I say it's better just to break a body part. Look at these photos on my wall.' He waved his hand, drawing a half-loop with cigarette smoke. 'I'm a respected member of the community. My connections go way up. I am not afraid of anyone, especially not a little man like Zhang Hong. Gamblers make me sick. They have no backbone and no loyalty.' He paused, enjoying the sound of his own words.

Mei looked around the room. On the walls were photos of smiling faces, Big Papa Wu's amongst them.

'Then why did you go to his hotel?'

'I don't have to tell you anything.' He tapped his cigarette over the glass ashtray. 'But let me make one thing clear. He was already dead when I got there. Maybe he didn't kill himself. Maybe it was the gambling house. I don't know and don't care.'

'Don't you think the police may care?'

Big Papa Wu snorted. 'Do you know how many people travel to Beijing every day? Twenty thousand. Then there are the migrant workers who are here illegally. We are talking hundreds of thousands of off-the-book nobodies. Why would the police care about any of them? People die, that's just a fact of life.'

'So why did you tear the hotel room apart?' Mei looked at Big Papa Wu from beneath her eyelashes.

'Maybe I just didn't like his face. Miss, you have a pretty face and maybe a pretty mind inside that head of yours. Why don't you tell me what you are looking for, then I will tell you what I was looking for?'

Mei crossed her arms. 'What's in it for me?'

'Money, of course – why else would you be doing it?'

Mei stood up. Her back was hurting from the hard chair and her legs needed stretching. She idled her way along the wall of photos.

'How long have you been in this business?' she asked. Most of the photos had captions, but none was dated. Judging by the fashions, some of them had been taken years ago.

'Seventeen years.'

'Have you always been in Liulichang?' She recognised the pop star Tian Tian.

'No, I had other little shops here and there for a while. I moved to this one a few years ago.'

The last photo was black and white, taken at the time when Big Papa Wu was young and lean. His left arm was locked together with that of another young man, tall with handsome eyes and shy lips. Unlike Big Papa Wu, he had a quiet and almost withdrawn demeanour. An older man stood behind them, smiling proudly.

Mei stopped in front of the picture for a long time. She thought that she'd seen the older man before somewhere. But the harder she tried, the slower her mind seemed to turn until it finally jammed. She gave up.

'Where was this picture taken?'

She turned around to look at Big Papa Wu. His hair was shorter and no longer full. The flame inside his eyes had died.

'At my first store. That's my partner,' said Big Papa Wu casually. 'We were together "up mountain, down countryside". When I came back to Beijing, I had no job or home; he and his father helped me to set up this business.'

Big Papa Wu took in a long puff and then let it out slowly. 'Do you know why I am a good antiques dealer?' he asked suddenly.

'Why?'

Big Papa Wu shifted in his chair. 'Before I was a sent-down youth, I had been a member of a youth gang for some years. I thought I was tough. The thing about street gangs was that you never trusted anyone because none of us was trustworthy. We were all thugs. If you wanted to survive, you always had to watch your back.

'But things were different in the mountains of Dongbei. Our

camp was a patched-up old timber station deep inside the forest. In the summer we cut down trees and sent the logs down river. Winter was harsh, long, with deep snow. We were all teenage kids from Beijing. We had never hunted animals, never held rifles, never been cut off by snowstorms before.

'When you have to face the power of nature, you learn to trust. Not blind trust. Humans can be much more dangerous than wild animals. But you find out just who you can trust. You needed to know who would save you if you were in danger and who you could give a rifle to and not worry when you turned your back. Most importantly, you needed to know who you could speak your heart to without being betrayed to the Party secretary. Everything was empty out there – the landscape, the days and nights. If you couldn't talk to someone, you'd go crazy.

'The mountains were vast and deep. It was the kind of place that gave you the creeps because you knew you couldn't get out. Every winter, when the isolation and hardship got to be too much, someone would lose it and try to escape. But no one ever walked out of there alive.

'Like I said, there were dangers everywhere. One summer a boy we called Four-eyes, because he wore glasses, was swept away by the river. It had rained for many days.

'Winter was unbearable. Sometimes the supply trucks couldn't come to the camp for weeks because of the snow. It drove people mad. It drove them to do anything to get out. I mean, *anything*. I've seen the most innocent beings turn into devils.

'This is my point. I learned very quickly how to judge people – to work out who was truthful and loyal and who was not. Later on, a man we called Big Brother taught me to read face. You see, most dealers on this street know more about antiques than I ever could. But they can't read face. They don't understand people. But me, I know in an instant whether someone is lying.

'Now tell me . . .' Big Papa Wu leaned back in his chair, folding his arms across his chest. 'What's a pretty girl like you doing around here, looking for trouble?'

'What trouble?' Mei looked straight at Big Papa Wu and shrugged her shoulders. She didn't like being threatened.

'Miss . . .?'

'Wang.'

'Miss Wang, tell me something else. Do you trust easily?'

She watched Big Papa Wu's cigarette smoke dissolve out of the open window. She thought of Uncle Chen, the man whom she'd known all her life. He was the warm hand she held on to as a child and the uncle she never had. Thirty years of love was worth a lot of trust. Yet she had wondered, inside the long dark corridor of No. 309 Hospital, in a fleeting moment of doubt, just how well she really knew him.

At that moment, the telephone rang.

Big Papa Wu sapped his cigarette. 'Hello? Oh, fine . . . no sweat . . . really.' A trace of a smile crept over his face.

Mei wondered what her answer would have been if the telephone had not interrupted them.

When he hung up, Big Papa Wu was in good humour. 'Think about my offer. Perhaps you and I could do business. We find whatever it is together and I will make it worthwhile for you.'

Mei smiled. She laid one of her business cards on his desk and said, 'We'll meet again.'

31

Monday was humid. Like all Mondays, this one was a drag.

There was nothing of interest happening in the office. A couple of bills and a couple of harmless inquiries that would almost certainly end nowhere. No one called about the scar-faced man who had left his body in the Hotel Splendour, least of all the police. It was just a normal day, of no particular importance, a day the factory of life had been producing without change, week after week since factories began.

Mei read the newspapers. As usual, the *People's Daily* had plenty of editorials announcing government policies. Some of the same editorials were republished in the *Beijing Daily*. Even the normally informative *Beijing Morning Post* had only happy news to report – prosperity and the great expectation of Hong Kong being returned to China.

Mei binned the newspapers and walked out to the entrance hall. Gupin smiled at her from behind his computer. He was sharpening pencils and lining them up neatly on the desk like missiles.

'It's going to rain today,' he said.

Mei nodded. 'It looks like it. Could you call up the Research Institute of Mining and ask for someone who may know what the eye of jade is?'

Gupin had already reached for the phone when suddenly he stopped.

'Do you not mean *who* the eye of jade is?'

'Who?'

'Yeah, that's what we say in Henan. The jade is the emperor's stone, so the eye of jade meant a spy from the royal palace. Now we use the term for anyone who is spying for someone higher up, like the boss.'

Mei stared at Gupin, her mind racing. Luoyang is the capital of Henan and the capital of thirteen ancient dynasties.

Gupin watched her nervously. 'Sorry, that's not what you meant. I will make the call straight away.'

Mei was roused from her thoughts. Suddenly she remembered where she had seen the older man who was in the picture on Big Papa Wu's wall.

'It's all right. Forget about the call.' She smiled and said, 'Thank you.'

32

Uncle Chen lived in an apartment tower on Fuchang Gate Avenue.

It was lunch time. Cyclists of all ages were coming from all directions, dismounting and sending up clouds of dust. High school kids in uniforms arrived like athletes. Everyone was in a hurry to get home for lunch.

The noise in the street rose. Cars and trucks rumbled. White and blue electrical buses, looking like slugs with two black antennae, struck sparks from the overhanging wires.

Mei had to drive slowly, her car crawling behind bicycles, choking on its own exhaust. The cyclists either ignored her or glanced back with contempt.

Finally she found a parking spot at the side of Uncle Chen's building, which was flanked by two identical black and grey structures.

These towers had been built in the late 1980s. At the time of their construction, with their lifts and windowed corridors, they were the most desirable residential buildings in Beijing.

Today they looked like shrivelled prostitutes flaunting their overused bodies on the footpath. Passers-by spat on them, calling them ugly.

A crowd had formed in front of the lift.

'Come by for a hand of poker tonight?' shouted a beefy man standing behind two fashionable girls in high heels.

A man with glasses glanced at his wife, who pretended to be meditating on the balding head in front of her. He gave his neighbour a bitter smile: 'Maybe not.'

When the lift came, people packed in, hot and sweaty. One of the fashionable girls got her skirt stuck between the beefy man's legs, and he turned to smile at her. She yanked the skirt out and cursed, whispering something to her girlfriend. They both turned their faces away in disgust.

Mei got out on the tenth floor. Down the hall, a locked bicycle leaned against the grimy window. She peered out. Dark clouds thickened at the horizon. To her left, along a yellowing wall, she saw closed doors, some covered with iron plates. A delicious smell of cooking leaked from one of them.

Mei rang Uncle Chen's doorbell. She heard heavy steps and locks turning.

'Mei, what a surprise!' Uncle Chen held the door open and stood to one side.

His entrance hall was small and taken up by a bulky washing machine. A washing line hung from a nail on the doorframe.

'We are having lunch,' said Uncle Chen. 'Have you eaten? Would you like to join us?'

'No, thanks. I'm not hungry.' Mei shook her head. She was nervous. Every move she made seemed false. Her smiles were forced, her voice unsteady, and she didn't know where to put her hands.

Auntie Chen came out of the living room, chopsticks in hand. Her face was covered in beads of sweat.

'Mei, you poor child.' Auntie Chen leaned towards her as if she was grief-stricken; her plain face had come to life. 'But of course, we shouldn't lose hope. I have a feeling that your mother will pull through. We all pray for her.'

She ushered Mei into the living room.

Mei sat down on the sofa and looked around. The flat had been decorated with much effort by someone of limited means. A bookshelf stuffed with family photos, books and ornaments stood in the corner. Against one wall was a single bed with a green and cream bedcover. It was Auntie Chen's. On the next wall, forming an L-shape, was the bed belonging to Uncle Chen. A few pots of flowers, books and miscellaneous household items cluttered the windowsills. Hanging from a wire at each side of the window were gold velvet curtains.

'I'll be done soon,' said Uncle Chen, shovelling food hastily into his mouth.

'You sure you don't want some tea?' asked Auntie Chen.

'I am fine. Don't worry about me,' said Mei.

'Okay, I'm done,' said Uncle Chen, standing up. He was still chewing. 'Let's go.'

'Why leave? You two can chat here. I'll do the washing up in the kitchen.'

'I need to get back to work early. Mei and I can talk on the way.'

'What about your nap?'

'Not tired anymore,' said Uncle Chen, avoiding his wife's gaze.

'Then wait a moment.' Auntie Chen went quickly to the kitchen, returning a moment later waving a shopping bag. 'Buy some radishes on your way home. We'll have hotpot for dinner.'

Uncle Chen took the bag and nodded.

'Goodbye, Auntie Chen,' Mei said. 'We'll chat next time.'

The streets were now quiet. It was siesta time. Most vendors had boarded up their stalls. Drivers of flatbed carts had parked under the trees and were squatting in a circle eating their packed lunches.

Uncle Chen walked beside Mei, pushing his bicycle. 'Sorry, so hot and humid out here. But you know your auntie; it's better she doesn't hear what we say.'

There was a stone bench under an oak tree, a body slumped over it. Someone had found a bed there for the next hour. Further on they came across a bench that was not occupied, and sat down.

The sky threatened to rain.

'Uncle Chen, you've been my family's friend for a long time. You've known me since I was little. So I'll just come straight out and say it: I assume you had your reasons.'

Mei had toyed with many alternatives, yet the words that came out were unrehearsed.

'You never went to Luoyang, did you? Otherwise you would know what the eye of jade is – or, more precisely, *who* the eye of jade is. It was my mother and Song who had that assignment and it was my mother who told you about the jade seal. You came across the article on the ceremonial bowl by chance. It made you think. Maybe you thought there was a chance for you to get rich, maybe you had other motives. But why lie to me?'

Uncle Chen's face reddened. He took out a crumpled handkerchief and wiped the sweat from his brow. 'I'd never—'

'Now I know why you didn't want me to tell my mother.' Mei stared at Uncle Chen. All the anger and sense of betrayal bottled up inside her threatened to burst out. 'Were you pleased that she had the stroke? Now she may never know who you really are.'

'Please, Mei, don't say such hurtful things. You don't know how much she meant to me.' Uncle Chen gasped for air like an insect trapped in a spider's web. 'My weakness was that I always wanted things. I wanted to be someone, to have a good life. Don't I deserve that? I've always followed the orders of the Party. I gave my heart and never hurt anyone, at least not deliberately. But I was never good enough, not for your mother, not for my work unit and not even for my family.

'Look at my home, one hundred square metres. Is that the best I will ever have? One hundred square metres for a family of four. Your auntie and I have slept in the living room for so many years that it has become a habit. Dong Dong needs to wait till he gets married for his work unit to consider him for housing. Jing's work unit has no housing at all. They earn so little that they couldn't afford to buy or rent.

'I'm a college graduate. I used to think I could be brilliant. But look at Song; he's got three hundred square metres just for himself and his delinquent son. That little bastard is a worm and Song knows it. But Song bails him out every time. Why? Because he can! He's got power and connections and his son rides around town chasing women in a chauffeur-driven car.

'My children don't do drugs, they don't run with criminals, but they have nothing, because their father is nothing. Who am I? I'm a nobody and your mother knows it.' His head dropped into his hands.

Mei didn't say anything. There was no need to.

'Sorry, Mei,' he sighed. 'I never intended for you to find out. I went to you because I knew that you wouldn't question me.'

'Yes, I was a fool to believe your lies. What else did you lie to me about? Did you send my father to prison? Did Song Kaishan do it? How did my father die?'

'I've told you all I know, Mei. That's the truth. I came to you because I wanted both of our families to profit. I thought we'd share the money.'

'What money?' Mei said. 'The jade seal was most likely destroyed long ago, and you know it. So I asked myself why you started this. I think you did it for revenge. You knew I would track it down to Song. You came to me because I was the right person to do it. I am my mother's daughter. Now it's my turn to do the talking for a change. Get me a meeting with Song.'

'You won't get into the Ministry without security clearance.'

'But you can. Tell him I need to talk to him and soon.'

Back in her office, Mei sat by the phone. From her window she watched the clouds brewing a thunderstorm.

She called Lu and left a message with her assistant. She wondered whether Lu's doctor friend had found out anything from the hospital.

Gupin went home. It was getting dark. Finally, the telephone rang.

'He will see you at the Three Red Flags Bar in Hohai in an hour.' Uncle Chen's voice was tight and dry. There was a moment's hesitation. 'Mei, don't go. Let's forget about the whole thing.'

'I'm afraid it's too late for that,' she said.

33

The sky was like a giant black lid poised to drop. Lightning came in waves, chased by thunder. Rain slanted down sideways.

Mei stepped on the accelerator hesitantly. She couldn't see the road or the canal. Walls of water slashed on her windshield and in front of her headlights. In a flash and a roll of thunder she saw the dark, arching shape of a stone bridge. Red lights flared in the blackness ahead as she inched forward. At the next flash she made a turn and saw the bars of Hohai, lit up like paper lanterns in a stormy sea.

Mei left the car by the bridge and got out. She tucked her head down, leaning her shoulder against the rain. Straight away her shoes were soaked, her jeans soaked. Water was leaking into her sleeves as she tried to hold on to her raincoat.

She saw the black Audi, clinging on to the slope running down to the canal. She walked on. Something or someone was moving inside the yellow windows, but she couldn't see clearly. The rain had obscured everything.

When she saw the Three Red Flags Bar, she crossed the road.

There was no one about, no tourists, no policemen on duty or waitresses to invite you in. No one was offering special drinks or happy hour.

Mei battled against the wind and rain to the door. When she was about a foot away, she made a final push and reached the doorknob.

It turned and she fell into the bar. The manager rushed over to shut out the storm.

A heavy metal band was playing. The lead singer, in a primeval outfit, jumped and screamed as if she had springs for legs. The guitarist, with spiky hair and tight jeans, was cool. She played as if she didn't care, and probably she didn't. The drummer was a whirl of flying hair.

The manager said something that Mei couldn't hear. She wondered whether she'd come to the right place. She peeled off her raincoat and gave it to the manager, who handed the dripping yellow plastic garment to a waitress in black.

'I'm here to see Mr Song Kaishan!' shouted Mei as loudly as she could. She put all her strength into the name, hoping that he would hear it.

The manager's mouth opened. Mei thought that he shouted back, but she didn't hear what he had to say.

He gestured for her to move away from the band. At the side there was a rosewood door with two leaves, each decorated with intricate carvings from top to bottom.

'This way,' she heard him say, and followed him through it.

The corridor was narrow and lined with dark wooden panels. They seemed to have walked around the house to the back. Here only the sound of the drumbeat could be heard.

'Please.' The manager opened a door and indicated for Mei to enter. 'Mr Song, your guest is here,' he said crisply and, with a click of the doorknob, he was gone.

It was a windowless room. A low black table sat in the middle surrounded by soft cushions. Neon pink lights glowed from the edges of the ceiling.

Song Kaishan sat on the cushions behind the table. In front of him was a number of small plates of salted eggs, marinated pig's earlobes and roasted peanuts. There was a bottle of *Wu Liang Ye*, its trademark red and white colours instantly eye-catching. A white porcelain liquor warmer had been lit next to it.

'I got here early. I hope you don't mind.' He pointed at the layout on the table.

Mei couldn't tell how long he had been drinking or how much. The room smelled strongly enough of rice wine to intoxicate a pig. Song extended a white hand and motioned for Mei to sit down. His rimless glasses added to the intelligence of his looks as well as acting as a screen for his thoughts.

'I hope you're pleased with what I've done for your mother.'

Mei felt herself sinking as she lowered her body into the cushions and curled up her legs. She knew that she ought to be grateful to Song, maybe say a word or two of thanks. It wasn't difficult to be gracious in front of an elegant man. But she didn't want to be.

'I didn't come to talk about my mother. I'm here because of a jade and a man called Zhang Hong.'

Nothing changed in his expression.

'Would you like to hear the story?' Mei asked.

Song slowly filled up the liquor warmer. A sharp smell of rice wine rose like smoke.

Mei carried on. 'Thirty years ago, two young secret agents were given a field assignment to Luoyang, the ancient capital, where tens of thousands of members of the Red Guard had taken it upon themselves to smash the old traditions – museums, books and the lives of intellectuals – and in doing so had broken into factions and were fighting amongst themselves. The agents' job was to provide support to the Red Guard as well as collecting intelligence on anti-Mao feelings in the province.

'One of the faction leaders was a teenager named Zhang Hong, a real brute, and a gambler by nature. Maybe he had seen one of the agents taking a valuable jade from the museum, so he grabbed one for himself: a Han Dynasty ceremonial bowl. Zhang Hong knew nothing about antiques, but he was not entirely stupid.

'Thirty years later, everything has changed. Revolutions have long gone out of fashion. Now, money rules. So Zhang Hong came to Beijing to sell the ceramic he had stolen from the old Luoyang Museum. Instantly he was rich.

'What would someone like Zhang Hong do when he has money? He spends it. He lived a life that he never could have dreamed of. He picked up a girl from a night café and went to stay at a flashy hotel. They gambled heavily.

'Soon he lost all the money and was in debt. He went back to the dealer who had bought the ceremonial bowl asking for help. The dealer refused. By pure chance Zhang Hong saw a photo in his office and recognised the father of the dealer's business partner, who was in fact the agent he had seen in Luoyang thirty years ago.

'He decided to blackmail him. Then he was murdered in his hotel room.'

Song Kaishan poured a shot of rice wine for himself and another for Mei.

'Why are you telling me this?'

'It was not just the jade that he was blackmailing you for, was it? Stealing national treasures is a small crime compared to murder. There were many killings in Luoyang. How many were committed by your own hands?'

Mei looked at the shot cup but didn't touch it.

Song shook his head and laughed. He emptied his cup.

'Are you worried? You think I may have drugged your drink? Mei, you've got me all wrong. I loved your mother. Perhaps I'm still in love with her. Please, let me tell my story now that I've listened to yours. I've waited for thirty years. I've done her enough harm.

'The Cultural Revolution! Who didn't do something terrible in the Cultural Revolution? Many people killed people. But your mother couldn't stomach it.'

He poured himself another shot.

'Your mother always said that the best quality of your father was his integrity and courage. So he had courage, so what? Challenging the Party was not an intelligent thing to do, not during the Cultural Revolution. Look at what he brought you: the hard-labour camp. Your mother chose to go with him. Your father could offer her nothing – no protection, no food. Why did she go?'

'Because she loved him.'

'Maybe she needed to prove to herself that she loved him.'

Mei stared. Words hung heavily inside her throat.

'In any case, your mother could not afford to be as arrogant and selfish as your father. She had two young daughters to worry about. The reality was that you and your sister simply could not survive that kind of life. So she came back and asked me for help. It wasn't easy. She had sealed her own fate when she refused to cooperate with the Party and went off to the labour camp with your father. The Party never forgets or forgives.

'I helped her, at great risk to myself. She did what the Party asked of her and gave evidence against your father. She had to leave the Ministry, of course. Her marriage to your father and her conduct up to that point had disqualified her from the service. But by turning in your father, she saved herself and the two of you. I tried to help her as much as I could after she left the Ministry, finding her temporary jobs and accommodation. But in those years sometimes I couldn't even protect myself and my own family.

'Towards the end of the Cultural Revolution, when I was hard up myself, I happened to come across your father in prison. I had always known him as someone smart, cultured, if not a bit arrogant. So it was a shock to find him a broken man. To this day I remember him, sitting in the corner coughing, or limping around the prison yard. Whenever there was a loud noise or the guards came near, his eyes would twitch and his body would shrink. He was like a terrified bird trapped inside an invisible cage.

'I tried to talk to him as one prisoner to another. But your father didn't want to listen. He wasn't the kind of man who forgave easily. Hatred had planted roots within him which had grown deadly knots. I could see that it was killing him from the inside.

'I wasn't in prison for long. After a few months I was transferred, and I was released when the Cultural Revolution ended.

'It was not until I came back to Beijing that I heard about your father's death. The official account was that he had died of illness in prison. I went to see your mother. It was the only time that she agreed to see me. She wanted to know everything about him. What kind of food did he eat? Was he in good spirits? Was he thinking of the girls? What did he say about her? Why didn't he write? I didn't think she had ever had any information from him. So I told her everything. A lot of it didn't come as a surprise to her, but she still took it very hard. When I told her that your father had said that he would never forgive her, she cried.'

The elegant man paused, taking a sip of *Wu Liang Ye* to wet his throat. Mei thought that she saw sadness glistening in his eyes.

He drew a long breath and recovered.

'Have you met my son?' The corner of his mouth lifted in a bitter smile as Mei shook her head. 'You haven't missed much. He's a real horror, and he despises me. All he wants from me is the use of my car and protection whenever he or his pal Big Papa Wu get into trouble. I was told that this bar is one of his favourite haunts. We don't see much of each other these days. He goes out late chasing women and then sleeps all morning. I know that I have a bastard for a son, but what can I do? He's all I've got.

'In China what matters is power. Money couldn't get your mother into 301 Hospital, but I can, my power can. But power doesn't last. One day I will die and what then? What will happen to my son, without me to protect him? He won't survive prison. He could never tolerate suffering. He's one of those people with weak heads. In the Cultural Revolution, he was sent to the mountains to be re-educated. He might have died if not for Big Papa Wu.'

He tipped his head back, emptied what was left in his cup and wiped his mouth with a crisp white handkerchief.

'People like Zhang Hong ruin lives, their own and those around them. Someone had to take a stand. Our society is better off without people like him.

'Why are you looking at me like that? No, you can't judge me. You haven't the right. I did what I needed to do, just as your mother did what she needed to do. There was no room for morality at the time of the Cultural Revolution. You survived at any cost. You young people don't understand. You always act as if we were monsters.'

Song tried to push himself up. He wobbled as though there was something inside that he had lost, something he needed in order to steady himself. At the second try he got up slowly, with the care of a man who has had too much to drink.

'Please go and be with your mother. I talked to the hospital before I came. They told me that she was going to recover.

'Sooner or later our time will come. All we have left now is waiting. But you know what? This waiting has been harder than I thought. Every wrong you've done in your life catches up and eats into you. Maybe that's how we'll all go, when we have no heart left to suffer.'

He walked towards the door. Mei got up too, and reached out to help him.

Song pushed her away as if she were a morning rose, too thorny to touch. He straightened his body. His hands shook a little, but he was steady now.

'No, it doesn't matter. Not anymore. But I do want to protect my son and to leave him something that could set him up for a long time after I'm gone. I heard money is all you need in America.'

He grabbed the rosewood door and pushed open one of the leaves.

'Stop looking for the jade. It doesn't exist anymore.' He turned around. 'Chen is a coward, always letting other people do his dirty work. That is why your mother could never love him. But he hung around, always the shapeless shadow, the sensitive ear, always around. He's never gotten anywhere and never will. If he wants to get me, tell him to come and use his own hands.'

Mei watched him walk through the empty bar with small, precise steps. He held his back straight. When he came to the door he opened it and walked into the rain. The wind had slowed. His driver ran from the bank of the canal, holding up an umbrella to shield his boss.

34

Mei moved the chair closer to her mother's bed and sat down.

A tube was taped just below Ling Bai's nostrils. Long colour-coded cables like subway routes on a map linked her to a monitor with constantly changing numbers.

Though Ling Bai was much the same as when Mei had last seen her, Mei had a feeling that underneath the façade something remarkable had happened. She watched her mother sleep, her breathing quiet and steady. The expression of her face had softened. There was a kind of moisture, perhaps even a slight hint of colour, in her cheeks.

Mei sat and watched her mother for a while. Then she tiptoed to the window where Little Auntie was dozing.

Mei tapped her arm. 'Little Auntie,' she said, 'why don't you go home? I'll stay with Mama.'

Little Auntie opened her eyes. 'I'm all right. It's almost daybreak.'

Both of them decided to stay. Little Auntie added hot water to old tea-leaves in her cup and handed it to Mei. They sat by the window and shared the tea, separated by a generation and bonded by love.

Little Auntie pointed to the body in the other bed. 'Brought in a few hours ago. Suicide, a soldier.'

'Where is his family?'

'It doesn't look like he has family in Beijing.'

The body groaned a little.

Mei looked at her aunt. Like Mei, she had inherited the strong nose from their ancestors. Wrinkles had begun to claim her face. Veins spread across her arms and the backs of her hands like ivy.

Little Auntie did not notice Mei's gaze. She sipped tea and watched the lights change colour on the monitor. She didn't know how Mei's heart ached.

'Did you . . .' Mei started timidly, 'ever question?'

'Question what?'

'All that stuff that happened in the Cultural Revolution, the things you did and choices you made.'

'Of course we did. The whole nation questioned, for ten long years after the Cultural Revolution ended. But what's the point of dwelling on the past? No one can change anything.'

Little Auntie passed the cup to Mei. 'We were like sheep being herded around. We didn't have much choice.'

'Is that really true? Everyone made choices. Mama took us out of the hard-labour camp but left Baba there. Baba chose to believe in his ideals. Some people killed, some betrayed family and friends. We all make our choices.'

'But you can't compare what you have today with that of your ma or ba. We lived in a very different time. It was like a civil war, full of life and death. Most of the time we had no control.'

'But what if you had control? What if you knew that you were sending someone to die?'

'What are you talking about?'

Mei wanted so much to tell Little Auntie what she knew. But she could not say a word. The burden of her mother's secrets, now hers to keep, bore down on her. She was cursed. She had been raised on poisoned love and now her love was poisoned too.

Mei turned away, breathing hard. 'I don't know. Everything seems wrong. I always thought truth and love would make me happy. But they didn't. Now I have some difficult choices to make myself. Do I turn in a murderer who is my family's saviour? Ancient wisdom says one life is worth another in exchange, but what about justice? What about justice for the one we lost? Can we forgive an assassin even if she had the best reasons?'

Little Auntie looked at Mei, confused and worried. 'Who is this? Someone I know?'

Mei didn't answer. She returned the teacup to Little Auntie and walked to her mother's bed.

There, by the side of the woman who had given her life twice, she sat down. Mei laid her face on top of her mother's hand and felt the touch of her skin, warm and tender. Mama opened her eyes a little and then closed them again. Mei thought she saw a fleeting smile.

The night was as silent as her tears. She wondered whether love could be condoned without justice.

'I'm sorry, Mama,' she whispered.

From beyond the dark window, Mei heard the first cry of the morning bird. Soon the day would awake and morning would arrive like waves upon an unspoiled shore. Light would rise from behind the horizon. It would bring the touch of paradise.

POSTSCRIPT

In the summer of 1999, a Han Dynasty jade seal was sold in New York to an anonymous collector. The amount paid was never disclosed.

Acknowledgments

My deepest gratitude goes to Toby Eady, my agent and friend, for his vision, faith, wisdom and kindness.

I am grateful to Laetitia Rutherford for her intelligence that has made this book possible.

I thank Humphrey Price, Michal Shavit and Ali Lavau for their wonderful insight, advice and editing.

Finally, my thanks and affection go to my beloved Beijing, to my sister, my father and my friends.